THE

GREEN

BY

JUSTIN REICHMAN

www.scobre.com

Scobre Press Corporation
2255 Calle Clara
La Jolla, CA 92037

Scobre Press books may be purchased for educa-
tional, business or sales promotional use.

First Scobre edition published 2003.

Edited by Debra Ginsberg
Illustrated by Larry Salk
Cover Design by Michael Lynch

ISBN 0-9708992-9-7

www.scobre.com

To all the dreamers...

We at Scobre Press are proud to bring you Volume 9 in our Dream Series. In case this is your first Scobre book, here's what we're all about: The goal of Scobre is to influence young people by entertaining them with books about athletes who act as role models. The moral dilemmas facing the athletes in a Scobre story run parallel to situations facing many young people today. After reading a Scobre book, our hope is that young people will be able to respond to adversity in their lives in the same heroic fashion as do the athletes depicted in our books.

This book is about Jason Green, the class clown, a kid who spends most of his days trying to make people laugh. The problem is that he does it at his own expense. He makes fun of the fact that he is overweight and plays pranks that get him into trouble. He pretends to be someone he's not in order to be a part of the cool crowd.

The Green is a story about how the game of golf helps Jason figure out who he really is and who he wants to be. He learns that sometimes believing in yourself enough to *be* yourself is the hardest thing to do.

We invite you now to come along with us, sit down, get comfortable, and read a book that will dare you to dream. Scobre dedicates this book to all the people who are chasing down their own dreams. We're sure that Jason will inspire you to reach for the stars.

Here's Jason and *The Green*.

CHAPTER ONE

TROUBLE ON THE FLIGHT TO MARS

I can't say that I was totally surprised about ending up in the Puyallup Fair security shed dressed like an alien. But I certainly didn't plan on a huge—and totally insane—security guard named Officer Armstrong screaming at me so loud that a little blue vein popped out of his neck. And I definitely didn't plan on Officer Armstrong calling my mother and having her escort me out of the fair. It just worked out that way.

My name is Jason Green, I'm thirteen years old, and I guess you could say that I'm kind of a goofball. I go to the Puyallup Fair pretty much every October. It's been going on as long as I can remember. My parents went there when they were kids, which means the fair is really old, because they haven't been kids in like thirty years.

Puyallup is a rural town about an hour outside of Seattle. I've lived here my whole life. Puyallup is pronounced "phew-al-up." If you think it's hard to say, try spelling it. I get excited about the Puyallup Fair every year because it's got all kinds of great things, like skeet ball, roller coasters, and this cow made entirely out of butter—you have to see it to understand, trust me. But my absolute favorite thing about the fair is the Flight to Mars. It's this ride that's supposed to be like taking a trip to Mars and back. You sit in an electric car that goes around on this track and you pass by all these hokey glow-in-the-dark martians and giant robot spiders. There's fake fog and flashing lights too. The car jerks you around on the track, and sometimes you're facing backward so you don't know what's going to happen next. I must have ridden the Flight to Mars at least a hundred times.

A couple of months before the fair was supposed to open, I got this great idea in my head. What if I dressed up like an alien and found my way into the workings of the Flight to Mars? What if, at the perfect moment, I jumped out and scared some unassuming passengers? Funny, right? I thought that a screaming martian would add some flavor to a rider's experience. I almost felt like I was doing a service to the fair in some way. Almost.

I told my best friend Calvin about my plan and he also thought it was an excellent idea. In fact, he liked the concept so much that he assisted me in creating the perfect costume. We searched my house until we found the right gear. I put on some old silver ski clothes and colored my face green with glow-in-the-dark paint that was leftover from last Halloween. I made antennae with one of my mom's headbands and some glow sticks. To top everything off, I put on a set of gigantic fangs I'd kept from a spider costume I wore in a school play. I don't know if aliens actually have fangs, or if I looked even remotely like an alien for that matter. Either way, Calvin and I thought the costume was pretty scary. After all, I did have a green face and fangs. If I saw something with a green face and fangs, it would scare the heck out of me.

You're probably wondering how I managed to get into the fair dressed like an alien. Well, the Puyallup Fair has a whole bunch of weird characters walking around, making it easy to blend in. The best way for me to describe the fair would be to tell you what I saw on my way in. Directly in front of the entrance, there were two men wrestling each other in full scuba gear. A woman cheering them on was wearing a gigantic block of cheese on her head. She had just purchased some popcorn from a guy in a bear suit. He was on roller skates. In other words, the fair was like a giant freak show. So it made sense that nobody said a word when Calvin entered beside a green-faced alien with fangs.

By the time we were in line for the Flight to Mars I was so excited that I could hardly stand it. I was giggling uncontrollably, anticipating the scared reaction of unsuspecting passengers. Our car came up and Calvin and I hopped in. The guy loading us looked like he was working on an assembly line or something. He didn't even glance up at us, let alone comment on the fact that I was dressed as an alien. Our car sped away unnoticed.

When the car moved us into the darkness and just past the oversized stuffed green monster, I squeezed out of my seat.

"Good luck, man," Calvin said in a serious tone, bumping knuckles with me. "I'll see you outside."

"Thanks," I said.

I crossed the track and crouched down on the other side of the monster, out of sight from the mechanical cars slowly passing by. The first few came by, but they were filled mostly with laughing boys and kids with their parents. Then I heard them. The voices of two girls were coming my way. As they rounded the bend, I could see that they were alone and that they already looked freaked out. It was too perfect. I attacked. "Boo-ahhh-ha-ha-ha-ha!" I screamed as I jumped in front of their car.

Maybe my costume was too scary. Maybe my fangs were too realistic. Maybe my "boo-ahhh-ha-ha-ha-ha" sounded a little too convincing. Whatever the reason, the two girls absolutely freaked when they saw me. They started screaming and crying within a few seconds, so I immediately backed off and ran for cover behind the stuffed monster that I could barely find in the darkness. But even with me out of sight, they kept wailing away. They'd passed by and were far down the ride, but I could still hear them like they were right next to me. I knew this was going to mean trouble.

I figured that now was probably a good time to get out of the Flight to Mars as fast as possible. But the place was totally black, and finding the exit in the darkness was basically impossible. I started running and looking for a way out, but it seemed like with every step I took, I was bumping into something or tripping over a wire. First, I tripped on the track and fell into the giant robot spiderweb. I was caught and wrestled the web and the spider to get free. Something was blocking my arm, so I pushed forward as hard as I could until I heard a loud snap. A spider leg broke off into my hand and I was free. Unfortunately, the spider started making a hissing sound, and I began to smell smoke. Now, I really needed to get out of there.

I ran to my left but was stopped again by that stupid stuffed monster. And I mean literally stopped. I ran into the green giant at full speed and we both fell down. Frantically, I picked myself up and took off in the other direction. It was too dark to see where I was going, and my antennae kept getting into my eyes and blocking my vision. I knew it was only a matter of seconds before those girls reached the open air, and only a few more seconds until somebody came after me. My heart started to pound in my chest. I was sweating from the heat of my costume and the unnerving feeling of being trapped in the darkness. Finally, I saw the exit. But just as I bolted toward it, I tripped again and fell into a pile of fake toxic waste barrels. (At least I hoped they were fake.) I had just about freed my left leg from one of the barrels when the lights came on.

This was bad for a couple of reasons. First of all, I saw how everything in the ride worked. I saw all the wires, the fake martians, and the cheesy lights. I thought the Flight to Mars was dumb with the lights off, but it was pathetic with the lights on; it was basically a warehouse filled with bad props. The second piece of bad news was that I could now see all the damage that I'd caused, and it wasn't pretty. The bigger issue, though, was the guard who had burst into the ride and had found me right away. I didn't even have a chance to run. I was still holding a plastic spider leg under my arm when I felt his gigantic hand pick me up by the shirt. I could barely see through the thick clouds of smoke that had formed.

When I got outside, Calvin was nowhere to be seen, but the two girls I had scared were right out front. They were crying hysterically and their parents glared at me. Apparently, they didn't get my joke either.

"I guess scaring two little girls makes you feel pretty big, huh?" the father said as I passed. This was not going to end well.

The security guard, who had still forgotten to remove his hand from my neck, was a gargantuan bald guy with terrible breath. He was so big that he looked fake, like a statue or something. No one should be allowed to grow that large. His arms were the size of my legs. His legs were like tree trunks. I told him that he would be an excellent prop for the Flight to Mars, but I don't think he was amused. This was not the kind of person I wanted to make mad, but it seemed like every time I opened my mouth he became more agitated by me. He was pacing back and forth in the security shed, yelling. The small wooden structure shook with each footstep he took.

"Son," he screamed, "your entrance into this Fair is a contract between you and the community at large. When you pass through my turnstiles, you are consenting to play by my rules. This is my fair! It's been my fair for twenty years. During those years, not one person has ever left the Flight to Mars screaming their head off like that. Do you know why that is?" I shook my head and he continued, "Because no punk kid in a cheap excuse for an alien costume has ever gone berserk in my ride! What's with you? The damage you caused in there," he paused and let the veins on his neck pop out even more, "well, we're going to have to close the ride for at least a week. A week! How does that make you feel?"

I was sure that was one of those questions that you weren't really supposed to answer, so I just continued to sit silently. After what seemed like an eternity of yelling, Officer Armstrong made me give him my phone number and he called my house. When he hung up, he looked at me and said, "Your mother will be here in twenty minutes. And let me tell you, son, I would not want to be in your shoes right now." I never agreed with anyone as much as I agreed with Officer Armstrong just then.

You know how sometimes, like on the last day of the school year, you look at the clock and wish you could speed up time so that summer could start already? Well, I was sitting in Officer Armstrong's security shed trying to do the exact opposite. Among security monitors, lots of walkie-talkies, and a poster of a gigantic weight lifter that said, "I MAY NOT BE SMART, BUT I CAN LIFT HEAVY THINGS," sat a black-and-white clock. It was the old style, not quite digital, the kind where the numbers flip down like a tear-off calendar. Anyway, I was staring at that old clock while Officer Neck Vein watched over me, shaking his head and opening his eyes as wide as he could every once in a while to freak me out. Meanwhile, I was trying to do everything in my power to slow the clock down. I concentrated as hard as I could. I concentrated so hard it hurt. I wanted the clock to move backward. I needed more time to build a defense against the impending doom of Mom's arrival.

2:19

Gobackgobackgobackgobackgobackgobackgobackgo
backgobackgobackgobackgobackgobackgobackgoback...

2:20...Nuts.

It was no use. My mom was going to be here in ten minutes and there was nothing I could do about it. At least Officer Armstrong had stopped yelling at me. I think he got bored. There's only so many times in a half hour that you can tell a person that they're "never going to amount to a hill of squat."

Officer Armstrong was now staring intently at the security monitors, looking for more problems to solve. Man, did this guy take his job seriously. I imagined him sleeping in the shed so that he could be seconds away from averting any disaster that might come up at the fair. The funny thing about this was that with the exception of a really hot day that melted the butter cow two years ago, nothing bad ever happened at the fair. Today was probably the highlight of Officer Armstrong's security career.

As the clock flipped to 2:31, my mom walked into the security shed. Officer Armstrong stood up when he noticed her. "You must be Mrs. Green," he said.

"Unfortunately today, yes," Mom let out a small laugh. "I'm sorry my son was such a nuisance." She looked over at me when she spoke those words.

"I am too," said Officer Armstrong. "It has been a superlative number of weeks, and I'm sorry that your son spoiled an otherwise perfect fair. With the destruction of the Flight to Mars and those little girls that he scared to death—"

"You scared a bunch of little girls, Jason?" Mom was

not happy.

"Yes he did, in addition to breaking the robotic spider, the zombie martian, toppling the toxic waste barrels, bending the track in two places, and setting off the smoke alarm." Officer Armstrong was very serious, reporting my misbehavior in the way that a TV anchorman would deliver the nightly news. I was ready for him to tell Mom that there would be "more at eleven," but instead, Officer Armstrong said, "I am sure you are probably a wonderful mother, Mrs. Green, but we really had a problem with your son today."

"I understand," Mom said. "I know you have a very hard job to do. I wouldn't want to be in your shoes. Thank you, Officer Armstrong."

Officer Armstrong puffed up his chest like a dog being praised. "I'm just doing my job, Mrs. Green. I remember back in eighty-five when those boys tried to break in here after dark and shave the bearded lady." His eyes began to get watery as he finished the story. "When I walked into her tent, she was sound asleep and her face was already covered with shaving cream." He paused for emphasis, looking at Mom in the eye. "Luckily, I got there just in the nick of time."

Mom looked confused and ready to leave the shed when she said, "Well, I can assure you that Jason will be adequately punished for the trouble he caused today." My mom handed Officer Armstrong her business card. "And please, let me know how much money he owes to fix the ride."

Officer Armstrong took her card. "Thank you," he said. "I repeat, I'm sorry we had to meet under these circumstances."

"Me too," Mom said. "Come on, let's go, Jason." I stood

up, and Mom and I walked out of the shed together.

"Oh, and kid," I turned around as Officer Armstrong spoke to me, "if I so much as even see your face within one hundred yards of my fair, we are going to have a problem. Do I make myself clear?"

"Yes, sir," I answered.

As soon as we got out of earshot of Officer Armstrong, my mom let out a little laugh. "My goodness, he does take his job seriously."

"No kidding," I said. I was glad my mom was able to laugh this off. I could always count on Mom to see things in the same way I did. She knew that Officer Neck Vein blew this thing way out of proportion and that I didn't mean to cause any of the trouble that I did. She wasn't really going to punish me.

"You're grounded, Jason. Just because Officer Armstrong is a little nuts, don't think for a second that you are off the hook, young man. And you are in serious trouble this time." Well, so much for Mom seeing things the way I did.

We made our way toward Mom's car in absolute silence. As I passed the butter cow for the last time, I braced myself for what lay ahead.

CHAPTER TWO

GREEN'S ON THE GREEN

Most kids I know have one parent that goes easier on them than the other. If their dad says no to something, they go ask their mom. If their mom won't let them do it, they go to their dad. I remember when Calvin broke an expensive vase in his house about three years ago. Luckily, his mom was out of town. His dad took him to the store and made him pay for a cheap vase that looked like the expensive broken one. That was it. If his mom had been around, Calvin would probably still be grounded. I guess Calvin's dad is afraid of his mom too.

That's definitely not how it is in my family. My parents are exactly the same. They tell each other everything and they feel the same way about every issue. I'm not joking. Sometimes I feel like they have the same brain, or at least they share the same brain.

I sat at my desk writing a letter of apology to the family I scared. It had been a few hours since what I now refer to as the "alien incident." Let me recap what happened. The car ride home was strange. It was strange because my mom was silent the whole time. She said that she had a lot to think about, which I thought was just about the creepiest thing she could have said. When we got into the house I was sent up to my room while my parents discussed the situation in the living room. I don't think they know that I can hear everything they say when I put my ear up to the heating vent in my bedroom, but either way, here are some highlights from the conversation. It doesn't matter who was speaking, remember, my parents share a brain.

"I just don't know what we're going to do with him. It's not like this is the first time that he's done something like this."

"He's not a bad kid. I'm just afraid that if we don't do something major this time, he's never going to learn his lesson."

"Let's go for a walk."

After spending an hour staring at the wall, my parents came back from their walk and entered my room. They'd figured out my punishment, which was designed to teach me responsibility. Mom sat down in my desk chair directly across from me. Dad stood above her with his hands on her shoulders, shaking his head and raising his eyebrows every ten or twelve seconds.

Mom started out by telling me that I had to write a letter of apology to the family who "bore the unfortunate consequences of my senseless act." This letter was to be no less than

500 words and was to be approved by both parents before being mailed. So far, the punishment wasn't that bad. I could definitely handle writing a letter. But just as that thought passed through my head, I heard Dad sigh and Mom started to lay on the heavy stuff. She told me that I was grounded indefinitely. This meant no TV, no video games, not even comic books until Mom and Dad saw a "significant improvement" in my behavior. I was to go to school, come home, and do my homework. If I finished my homework, I was to go over it and check for errors. Until I proved to my parents that I could follow these rules, I would remain grounded. To quote my dad, "If you want to be grounded until you're eighteen, that's fine by us."

The third part, and definitely the worst part of my punishment, was that I was now part-time employed. Dad made a call to his friend who runs the Whispering Canyon Country Club, which is down the street from our house. I was to report in every Wednesday after school and all day Saturday and Sunday. I had no idea what this job was going to entail but I was very unhappy about it. I didn't want a job, especially not at a golf course. I hated golf!

Dad told me that I was going to start work next week. I was devastated. Mom and Dad never smiled brighter. They were sure that with all of these measures, I would learn responsibility and become a better person. Although I loved my parents and knew they were trying to help me, I was sure they were going about it all wrong. When I was asked if I had any questions, which I didn't, I was told to begin the first draft of my apology letter. They left my room and I felt like my life was over.

So there I was sitting at my desk, working on the letter. To be honest, it's pretty hard to write a good letter when you're not really that sorry. This whole thing was just a big misunderstanding. I didn't mean to scare the girls as much as I did, and I certainly didn't mean to break anything on the ride. It was all just a joke. I don't understand why no one else could see it that way.

The job punishment was the biggest one that I'd had, and I'd been punished a lot. I won't go into the whole "egg foo young incident," but let's just say this wasn't the first time my parents had been mad at me. I understand why they were making me write a letter, but the job at the golf course seemed a little excessive. I can't believe they were taking away my weekends!

When Mom saw the saddened look on my face later in the day, she said that it was all for the best and that she and my dad thought the job would keep me out of trouble. Oh yeah, and I haven't even told you the worst part yet. I didn't get to keep any of the money I would make! I had to buy the family of the girls I scared a bunch of expensive flowers and I had to pay for the damages I caused to the ride. The rest would go into a college fund.

And golf? What a dumb sport. I can't think of anything more stupid than the game of golf. All you do is hit a little white ball with a crooked stick, walk after it, then hit it again and walk after it again. Wouldn't it be easier to just throw the ball?

The next week of my life consisted of me trying as hard

as I could to figure a way out of this job mess. So far, all of my attempts have failed. And I've tried everything. Faking an illness didn't work—my mom can smell a faker right away. Plus, when I complained I had a fever, I held the thermometer to the light bulb too long when Mom wasn't looking. My mom said that it was impossible for me to have a 130-degree temperature.

Claiming that I had too much homework to work at a job fell on unsympathetic ears as well. To quote my dad once again, "If you have enough time to beat the princess or save the kingdom, or do whatever it is that you do with your video games, you've got enough time for part-time work." He had a point.

As a last resort, I constructed an argument against golf itself. I sat both of my parents down in the living room and made a presentation that I hoped would convince them that working at a golf course was not right for me. "As you can see from figure three, golf courses keep valuable, fertile land from growing soybeans," I said as I held up the charts I made.

I kept going despite my parent's glassy boredom. I delivered what I thought was a pretty convincing speech over the next twenty minutes or so. "In conclusion, golf is not an activity I can support morally. And, if I am not mistaken, the two of you have always encouraged, if not demanded," I was really getting into this, "that I stand for my convictions. I am against golf and therefore I can't, in good conscience, work at a golf course."

Not only did my parents deconstruct my argument point by point, but my mom made it clear that she and my dad were reaching the end of their patience.

"Jason," she said, "your dad and I are getting tired of this. If you would just spend half the time you spend trying to get out of this job thinking about your actions before you do them, you never would be in these situations in the first place. Also," she said as she handed back my presentation *Golf and the Soybean: The Silent War,* "and I'm not speaking just for myself here, stop with the handouts, and the e-mails, and the messages on our cell phones. You've made your position clear, but come tomorrow afternoon, you're showing up at work. There is no more discussion."

"Then I guess you don't want to hear what I have to say about the correlation between child labor and the increased chance of contracting the common cold?" I asked. My parents didn't even answer, leaving me standing in the living room with piles of papers and charts that ultimately only proved one thing—that there was no way I was getting out of this one. I couldn't stop Wednesday from rolling around any more than I could have stopped a runaway freight train.

Before I go any further, there are a few things you need to know about me. Despite hating the fact that I have to get a job, it's doubly worse that I have to work at a golf course. It would be just as bad if I had to work at a basketball stadium, football field, or hockey rink. You see, I hate all sports. You name the sport, and I'll hate it for you. I'll explain:

Basketball: Why do you have to always be dribbling the ball? It's so much easier to just run with the ball.

Baseball: There's this rule called the infield fly rule that Calvin tried to explain to me one time. It was the most ridiculous thing I've ever heard. Any sport that has a rule like that isn't for me.

Football: Any sport where you have to wear that much gear isn't really a sport if you ask me.

Soccer: Only using your feet is way too savage. What are we, Neanderthals? We use our hands in every single other thing we do in our lives. What's so special about soccer?

Tennis: What a crazy scoring system. What is 30-love all about? And deuce? Give me a break.

Swimming: I can walk faster than people swim.

Cross country: Why run when no one's chasing you?

I could keep going, but you get the picture. Sports are stupid. And golf is the granddaddy dumbest of them all.

As a result of my sports aversion, and probably some bad genes somewhere in my family tree, I have what you might call a little bit of a weight problem. My parents like to say that I'm big boned, but they're not fooling anyone. I'm a big boy and I know it. I'm not so fat that no one can sit next to me on the bus because I take up the whole seat, but I'm definitely not buying my pants in the kids' section either.

Over the years I have developed a strategy to divert attention away from my weight problem—it's pretty simple, really. All I do is make fun of myself before anyone else has a chance to. I have a T-shirt that says "CAUTION: WIDE LOAD" and I wear it at least once a week. Whenever the school year starts and I have to introduce myself, I always say something like, "Hi, my name is Jason Green. I spent the summer at weight-loss camp, but as you can see, I was the only one there who wasn't a loser." That always gets a big laugh. But when the laughter dies down, I'm left feeling pretty bad about myself. I guess that's why I'm always doing things that get me into trouble. I feel like if I can make people laugh, maybe they'll forget about what I look like. I know it sounds stupid.

When I think about being fat, for the most part it doesn't bother me. Sometimes, though, it makes me a little sad. Like if I watch a movie and some real buff guy is in it, I think that maybe I don't have to look this way. Also, although I talk to girls all the time, and I'm friends with lots of them, I've never had a girlfriend. Calvin's already gone out with four girls this year alone! Girls think I'm funny, but I've never been to a school dance or anything.

I'm pretty happy person, though, especially if I don't stop and think about things too hard. Plus, being heavy is way better than being a jock. I should know, because most of my friends are jocks. My best friend, Calvin, is the star of the football team. He's one of the leading receivers in the county. Because he's so good and because girls think he's so cute, Calvin's one of the most popular guys in school.

This has worked out very well for me. If I knew that when Calvin and I became friends when we were six years old that it would be my ticket into the popular crowd, I wouldn't have believed it. It's like I won the popularity lottery or something.

When Calvin and I are walking down the street, it's got to be a pretty funny picture for people who don't know us. Calvin is tall, muscular, good-looking, and cool. Man, is Calvin cool. He's got this cool walk and he dresses in cool clothes. He acts like he's older than everyone, he's bigger than everyone else, and he's hairier than everyone too. And then there's me. I look like a big clown standing next to Calvin. I'm short, fat, and I dress funny. I already told you about my "WIDE LOAD" T-shirt. I'm also partial to wearing suits. You can get a pretty cheap suit at your local thrift store. I have seven that I wear regularly. Combine that with my hair, and I've developed quite a unique look. My hair isn't really hair at all, it's more like the synthetic fabric used to make stuffed animals with. It's like a plush carpet, and it's shaped funny (I think I have an odd-shaped head). It's beyond a brush. My hair and I have an agreement. I let it do its thing and it doesn't say anything when I hide pencils in it.

Had I not been friends with Calvin, I'd probably be the guy getting beat up everyday. I'd be the freaky kid that the cool kids would give wedgies to in gym class. But instead of that, I'm the funny fat kid who hangs out with all the jocks. It's like some weird twist of fate.

Sometimes though, I feel like I'm not supposed to be

me. Like some kind of popularity mistake has been made some-where, and I'm living on borrowed popularity time. I'm sure that sooner or later all the cool kids will find out that I'm just a regular loser and I'll have to eat lunch by myself in the corner rather than sit at the cool table, making Mark Brotherton laugh so hard that milk shoots out of his nose. But until that day comes, I just play along.

That's not to say that Calvin doesn't owe me anything. Calvin gets a lot of laughs because of the stuff I do. I'll do anything for a laugh. Hanging around with me is like having your own personal comedian. Plus, usually I'm the only one who has to pay the consequences for a joke. I guess that's how I ended up with a stupid job at a golf course.

I tried to explain this to Calvin during lunch one day. We were sitting in the mushroom, our school cafeteria. Every-one calls the cafeteria the mushroom because it has a huge roof that comes down to the ground on four sides and looks like a gigantic concrete mushroom. There's a permanent smell to the mushroom. It's a combination of our school's egg sandwiches, tater tots, a splash of body odor, and just a hint of cleaning supplies. I was eating my peanut butter and butter sandwiches, trying hard not to breathe in through my nose, when Calvin sat down next to me. As always, he bought his lunch and was eat-ing a hamburger and fries.

I turned to face him, prepared to get something off of my chest. "You know, we both should have gotten in trouble for the Flight to Mars thing. The way I see it," I said between bites, "is that you're just as much responsible for this mess as I am. I mean, you thought it was a great idea, you helped me plan it, and you even made the antennae."

"So?" said Calvin.

"So, you should have to take this job with me," I said.

"No way, man," said Calvin. "I can't miss practice on Wednesdays. And we got exhibition games on the weekends. Besides, golf is dumb."

Mark Brotherton, who was listening in on the conversation, chimed in, "Yeah, golf *is* dumb. Golf's dumber than Luc Pierre." (Luc Pierre is a French exchange student at our school. In actuality, he's not dumb at all, he just doesn't speak English. In fact, he's probably the best math student in the whole school. Mark thinks it's funny to make fun of him and does so at every opportunity. I think it's mean, but Luc Pierre jokes always get a pretty big laugh from most of the cool kids.) "Sucks to be you, Green." Mark continued, laughing like a big dumb oaf. "Green's gonna be spending lots of time on the green now." Mark laughed harder, as if that joke was the funniest thing ever said.

I tried to continue my conversation with Calvin, but Mark wouldn't stop. He was singing now, "Green's on the green! Green's on the green! Green, green, Green, green! Green's on the green!" Most of the other guys at the table, and even some of the girls (this was the cool table, we sat with girls) were laughing and singing along. Remind me, why am I friends with these people?

I had to get them to stop, so I did the only thing I knew how to do well—make them laugh even harder. I stood up from my chair, unbuttoned my sport coat, and lifted my shirt up slightly to let my belly hang out. I grabbed a piece of lettuce from Sally Kornfield's salad, dipped it in her ranch dressing, and stuck it to my stomach. "No, this is greens on Green," I said. I didn't think it was that funny, but they were a pretty easy audience and probably in shock after seeing my hefty gut, so I got a good laugh. Once again, though, when the laughter died down, I felt kind of bad about myself.

The first bell rang and I stayed back as everyone else got up to go to class. I was upset that my friends were such morons, upset that I'd shown them all my fat stomach, and even more upset that Calvin wouldn't work with me. I was going to have to do this job by myself.

CHAPTER THREE

WHISPERING CANYON

After school the next day, I got on the bus that goes by the Whispering Canyon Country Club. It was going to be my first day of work. After about ten minutes of riding along a winding road and listening to Gary Taylor and Miguel Diaz argue about who would win in a foot race, I was ready to jump out the window.

"I'm faster than you, bro," Miguel would say.

"No chance," Gary would reply.

"I am, Gary. I'm like lightning," Miguel would retort.

"You're not, Miguel. I'm the lightning."

It went on like this for the entire ride. There's nothing more annoying in the entire world, trust me. By the time I got off at the right stop and walked into the Whispering Canyon Country Club, my head was killing me.

Up until this moment, I'd only been on a golf course

once, and that was when I was seven. My dad likes golf, so he tried to teach me. What a disaster that was. By the fourth hole, I threw three clubs into the woods. The first was an accident. The club slipped out of my hands, honest. But the second two, well, I just couldn't help myself. Needless to say, Dad never took me golfing again.

After the yellow bus escaped from view, I walked into the pro shop to look for Mr. Logan. Dad told me he was the manager of the course and the guy I'd be working for. I walked past a big display of clubs, racks of hats and visors, and buckets of golf balls leading up to the counter. A skinny kid was working the cash register. As I got closer I realized it was Eugene Jewel.

Eugene Jewel is in my class but I've never had very much to do with him. It's safe to say that he is not one of the cool kids. In fact, he's as far away from cool as I am from wearing a twenty-eight-inch waist on my pants. I guess you could say that there was something interesting about Eugene. You see, some kids aren't cool because they try too hard to be cool and end up looking like total dorks, but not Eugene. He never tries to be cool, and it doesn't seem to bother him at all.

Eugene came to our school last year. I guess being the new kid is always tough, but I think it's been especially hard for Eugene. I don't really notice him around school, and when I do see him in the halls or eating lunch, he's by himself. I've always felt like I should go up and talk to him, but then I think about what Calvin or Mark would say about me hanging out with such a weirdo, so I just leave him alone.

In my middle school we've got all kinds of kids. There

are dorks, nerds, cool kids, jocks, jerks, geeks, cheerleaders, brains, bullies, and brats. And then there's Eugene. I don't exactly know how to categorize him. He stays after science class to talk with Mr. Richards about different kinds of molds. Sometimes in the middle of class he'll just start laughing or he'll ask to be excused so he can check on the bugs he keeps in labeled jars inside his locker. I once saw him wear a T-shirt that said "I love gardening" on it.

I'd never really gotten a good look at him before today. He was hard to describe. He had this very awkward way about him that seemed to affect his every manner. He moved jerkily, like a robot. He was tall, probably a foot taller than I was, and super skinny. When I approached him, he was putting a bunch of tiny pencils into a small box next to the cash register. It was taking him a long time because he kept dropping the pencils. I walked up to the counter where Eugene was working and prepared to have our first conversation ever.

"Hey, you're Eugene, right?" I asked.

"Huh?" Eugene replied. He dropped a pencil on the ground as if I startled him when I spoke.

"You go to Challenger Middle School, right?"

"Yes."

"I do too. My name's Jason. You're in seventh grade, right?"

"Yes."

"Me too. You're new at school, right?"

"Yes. I moved here last year," he said. He wasn't being very talkative. I felt like I was making him nervous.

"So you work here?" I asked. What a stupid question.

Of course he worked here. People didn't usually just hang out behind the counter at pro shops.

"Yes. I work here part-time in exchange for free golf."

"You play golf?"

"Everyday," said Eugene.

Boy, this kid really was weird. No one plays golf everyday. "Well, I'm supposed to start work here today. I'm looking for Mr. Logan."

"Who?" he asked.

"Mr. Logan," I repeated. "The manager of Whispering Canyon."

"Oh, you must mean Harvey. I never knew his last name." He paused for a moment and stared at the ceiling. "You don't think of someone like Harvey having a last name. He's just Harvey."

"Yeah, well, I'm looking for Harvey Logan," I said.

"Harvey's fixing the green on hole five. If you want, I can take you there," he said.

"Sure."

"Hey Phil," said Eugene.

A huge man with curly blond hair, who was sorting a gigantic bucket of balls for a purpose I couldn't figure out, looked up, "Yes?"

"I have to go out to hole five. Can you please cover the register for me?"

"Sure," said Phil. He went back to sorting out his pile of golf balls.

Eugene led me around to the back of the pro shop. There were a bunch of white golf carts being charged. To me, getting

26

to drive a cart was the coolest thing about golf—really the only cool part about golf. I guess plaid pants are pretty cool too, but you don't need to play golf to wear them, and besides, plaid doesn't go too well with a suit. I asked Eugene if I could drive.

"Uh, you probably shouldn't. You don't know where hole five is, and it takes a little getting used to, driving the carts and all, and I don't think you've had any training, have you? You got to have a little training to drive the carts. I mean, it's not like driving a car or anything. I'm not old enough to drive, but it's a lot harder than riding a bike and it's a responsibility that you can't just get, you have to earn the responsibility." He continued, "Harvey made me wait six months before I could drive a cart. He didn't think I was ready when I started. He said that I wouldn't be able to handle the power of a golf cart. Besides, he always says the best way to learn a golf course is to walk it. So that's what I did for six months. I walked everywhere on the course. And he was right. I know the course like the back of my hand now. I still sometimes walk the course rather than drive the golf cart when I have the time. It's really neat to walk a course. I pretend like I'm playing and I plan out my shots. It's just probably best that I drive."

So Eugene drove the golf cart and I sat next to him. The whole time we were driving to hole five, he wouldn't stop talking. He just wouldn't stop. He reminded me of my aunt's golden retriever, Buttons. If Buttons was inside, he'd just lie around and be quiet all day long, but as soon as you took him outside, he'd go nuts. He'd run around barking, sniffing, and peeing on everything. Eugene wasn't peeing on anything, but he was acting like a different person as soon as we got outside, and he was very, very, very excited about golf.

"There's the dogleg left on hole one. It's pretty tricky. Sometimes I try to go over the trees and end up in the bushes. On hole two you have to drive over the second hill or your ball will roll back seventeen yards. Did you know that they used to play golf with round stones? Even though this is only a par three, it's the hardest hole on the course. I've only gotten par once, but Harvey says I'm getting much better. Golf spelled backward is flog, which is funny because you flog the ball. This is the second longest hole on the course. One time Harvey got in on only two strokes. It was great. Some pros can't even do that. Sometimes I pretend that golf balls are dinosaur eggs. At the bottom of the swing, a golf club can be going faster than two hundred miles per hour. Isn't the grass beautiful? It's a special blend that you can only find on this course. Harvey's a master of horticulture and can grow grass better than anyone else in the state. He lets me help him. I have a putting green I'm working on in my back yard. It's a work in progress, really."

With Eugene yapping in my ear about who knows what, we finally made it to hole five. I knew it was hole five because there was this little wooden sign that said:

Hole 5
Par 4
315 yds.

I also knew it was hole five because Eugene said, "We're coming up to hole five now. It would be the easiest hole on the course except for the green. The green on hole five is twice as big as any other hole. It's got sand traps in the front and back. The slope of the green makes a normally good shot end up in one of the traps. If you're not good enough to land close to the pin, you have to shoot off to the side of the green to play it safe. Otherwise you'll ping pong back and forth from sand trap to sand trap."

Thank you, Professor Golf. I had no idea what this guy was talking about. Doglegs, greens, slopes, pars, special kinds of grass…it was like he'd started speaking another language once we got into the golf cart. Did he really think I was interested in anything he was saying? I didn't say one word since he wouldn't let me drive, but Eugene had been going nonstop. This is what I figured out about him so far:

1. Eugene likes golf. A lot.

2. Eugene probably doesn't talk to many people.

3. Eugene thinks that Harvey is some kind of magical man.

4. Did I mention Eugene likes golf?

So the two of us walked up to the hole even though we easily could have driven. But Eugene felt that we'd get a much better feel for the entire hole if we walked it. I was starting to get a little annoyed. When he started talking again, he went on and on about how you have to square yourself up to the sand trap on this hole instead of the pin, and I reached my breaking point.

"Hey Eugene," I said as he mimed a club between his hands.

He looked up at me, "Yes?"

"I don't really know how to say this, so I'm just going to come out and say it." I stopped for a minute. "You see, I've never played golf before, so all this stuff that you're talking about doesn't make any sense to me."

Eugene looked at me like I was crazy. In Eugene's world, I guess everyone plays golf. I could tell he was thinking—his wheels were spinning. At first I thought he was going to get mad at me for not knowing golf, but after a few seconds this huge smile came across his face. "Well, I'll just have to teach you then."

"Great," I said.

CHAPTER FOUR

THE ANSWER'S IN THE BUCKET

Over by the flag on hole five, a man was kneeling on his hands and knees. He had a strange-looking tool in his hands and he was concentrating hard. Eugene and I got out of the cart and walked up to him. It was Harvey. I knew because Eugene had to call his name a few times.

"Harvey," Eugene said. Harvey didn't look up. "Hey Harvey." Eugene got a little closer to Harvey but there was still no reaction. "Harvey!" Eugene put a little more volume into it this time.

"Hello, Eugene," said an extremely calm Harvey, answering as if it was the first time he'd heard his name.

I stood awkwardly on the outskirts of the green, staring at the strange-looking man. When Harvey stood up I got an even better look at him. There were two things that I noticed about him right away. The first was that he was very short. He was a little shorter than me and I was only a kid. I'm already five feet tall, but hopefully I'll be about 6'2" when I'm done growing. That's how tall my dad is. The second thing I noticed about Harvey was his gigantic beard. It went all the way down to his shoulders. It was black and gray and seemed like it must have been growing his whole life. I pictured a young Harvey in kindergarten with his little black beard, carrying a lunch box and eating glue. You would think that his long beard would be accompanied by a thick head of hair, but you're wrong. Harvey was completely bald. The sun, which was barely shining through some heavy clouds, reflected off of his shiny head. His baldness and a pair of enormous ears made his beard even more dramatic. I have to say that I'd never seen anyone who looked quite like him.

As I got a closer look at his face, I was struck by his eyes. They were set deep in his face and were very dark, almost black. He was looking at me and it felt like he was looking into me.

"You must be Jason," he said. "I like your suit."

"Thank you," I said with a little smile. I liked Harvey right away, because nobody ever commented on my suits unless they were making a joke. I'd worn my blue suit on purpose today because it was my favorite. I wanted to make a good impression on my first day of work.

Harvey continued, "Well, Eugene and I are sure glad to be getting a little extra help around here." He paused, "Before you start, let me ask you a question."

"Shoot," I said.

"Look down the fairway to the flag at hole six over there," Harvey said as he pointed down the course. "Now, I want you to tell me what you see."

"Excuse me?" I asked. What did he think I would see?

"Look down the fairway to the pin." I knew the pin was the long stick that was attached to the flag, but I had no idea how I was supposed to answer this question. Harvey repeated his request. "I want you to tell me what you see when you look to the pin."

I answered, unsure of myself, "I see a bunch of grass, some water, some sand, some darker grass and a flag." Was this guy nuts?

Harvey closed his eyes for a moment. He opened them and looked into me again. "Thank you. Please go to the clubhouse and help Phil clean the range balls. Eugene, let's decide on the hole placement." Eugene and Harvey both got down on their knees and started looking for a good placement for the hole. They were completely ignoring me.

I felt like I had gotten something wrong, like I failed a test or something. "I also saw a bunch of bushes. I forgot to tell you about the bushes." They were both looking up at me as if *I* were crazy. "Did I not see something?" I asked.

"It is not what you didn't see, it's what you saw. You saw too much. Now, please help Phil. We do not have enough clean range balls." I hung my head for a moment and made my way toward the golf cart that was parked in the middle of hole five. Just as I was about to hop into the driver's seat, Harvey shouted out, "Jason, walk back to the clubhouse. You'll learn the course better that way."

So Harvey and Eugene starting talking about the proper placement of the hole while I walked back to the clubhouse to help Phil scrub some golf balls.

This is pretty much how things went along for the next two weeks or so. I would show up to work; Eugene and I would go find Harvey somewhere on the course; on the way over, Eugene would talk my ear off about slices, hooks, club selection, and how he can actually see the wind. He would also talk a lot about Harvey. From the way Eugene talked, you'd think Harvey was a superhero or something. Harvey could do this, Harvey could do that, Harvey could predict the weather, Harvey could smell where a ball landed, Harvey could talk to the squirrels.

Each day, we'd find Harvey on the course and he would ask me "The Question." Inevitably, I would give him the wrong answer. I didn't even get closer. Sometimes I would make things up that I saw, like a red bird or a giant ant. Harvey would shake his head and tell me to go to the clubhouse and help Phil. And I've got to tell you, I was getting pretty sick of Phil. Phil was a very tall, very skinny man whose ability to have a normal conversation was almost as bad as his ability to put on deodorant. Man, did Phil smell. It was unlike anything I've ever smelled before. He smelled like a combination of feet and grape soda. I used to like grape soda, but I don't think I can ever drink it again thanks to Phil.

The act (or art, as Phil says) of cleaning a golf ball is the most boring thing I've ever done. Phil and I would sit next to one another with a gigantic bucket of golf balls between us.

We each had a little bucket in front of us and a special rag that Phil called a chamois (pronounced shammy). I'd grab a golf ball out of the big bucket and put it in the little bucket, which was filled with cleaning solution. Then I'd scrub the golf ball with an old toothbrush. (I can almost guarantee you that it wasn't Phil's old toothbrush, he didn't strike me as the kind of guy who owned one.) Once all the dirt was scrubbed off, I had to dry the golf ball with the chamois. Then, I had to show it to Phil. This was where it got weird. Phil would actually study the golf ball. He'd close one eye and hold the golf ball in front of his face the way a jeweler studies a diamond. He'd do that for a minute, then hold it up to the light, like he could see through the ball or something. There'd be this moment of silence and then Phil would give me a letter grade. That's right, he would actually grade me on how well I cleaned a golf ball.

If the ball got an A- or higher, he'd toss the ball into a bucket of clean golf balls. Anything lower than an A-, he'd hand back to me to clean again. He'd usually give a comment like, "B plus, I can see a piece of dirt on dimple four hundred thirty-seven," or "C, not white enough," or my favorite, "D, if you can't see why, you've got no business cleaning golf balls."

I once asked Phil how long he'd been cleaning golf balls. He replied, "Cleaning things is a lifelong endeavor. It is my reason for being here." I guess he didn't include his own body in his mission to make the world a cleaner, better-smelling place.

By about the third week of hanging out with Phil, I had taken about as much as I could handle. First of all, I wasn't doing a very good job cleaning. I had at best a B- average. I think Phil had unusually high standards for golf ball cleanliness, but he showed no signs of lightening up. I was getting sick and tired of rewashing, rescrubbing, and re-chamoising golf ball after golf ball.

Although I wanted my weekends back and certainly didn't like sitting around cleaning golf balls with Phil all day, something about Harvey and Eugene and the game of golf was starting to intrigue me. I wasn't going to tell Mom and Dad this, though. Instead, I made them feel guilty about making me work, complaining about the beating my hands were taking from all that cleaning. I revealed my peeling skin to Mom, trying to get some sympathy that might lead to a few of the other sanctions against me to be lifted. But I had no such luck. Mom just laughed, telling me that I had dishpan hands and that I should use some yellow gloves if I wanted to keep them young and healthy looking.

Despite being interested in Harvey and Eugene, I couldn't take Phil for much longer. He was just too strange for me. From out of nowhere he'd start talking about the weirdest stuff. "Did you know that streetlights are actually video cameras? That way the government can watch us at night when we're driving. Ever wonder why you never see the president with his shirt off? It's because he's a robot designed by aliens. The aliens have puppet regimes all across the universe. You never see the president in the rain either, because he could short circuit. If you put your ear close enough to a worm, you can hear what it's thinking. Most of the time, it's thinking about eating dirt. The rest of the time it thinks about other worms."

I couldn't take it anymore. I knew that I was going to

be cleaning balls with Phil until I started answering Harvey's questions correctly. It was like some secret club that I couldn't enter without the password. When I walked to find Harvey at the beginning of each workday, I would stare down the fairway of each hole toward the pin. I was searching for the answer to Harvey's riddle. What would a golfer see? I asked myself. The truth was, I had no idea. Finally, I asked Eugene for some help. "Hey Eugene," I asked. "Why do I always get Harvey's question wrong? What does Harvey expect from me?"

"I don't think that you're looking very deeply into what Harvey's asking you."

"So that's why I'm stuck cleaning all day with Phil?"

Eugene continued, "I think Harvey wants you to have a golfer's mind before he starts giving you more complicated jobs away from Phil. It's kind of like he's training you."

Training? For what? I just wanted to know the answer. "Just tell me the answer, Eugene, will ya?"

"Well, maybe if you go further under the question you'll get to the real meaning behind what he's asking."

"What do you mean?" What was Eugene talking about?

"Well, for instance, when Harvey asked you to look down hole six, what did you see?"

"I saw a bunch of grass and stuff."

"Do you think that's what a golfer would see?"

"Of course. Unless the golfer was blind."

"Really?" asked Eugene. "You think a professional golfer looks down the fairway and just sees a bunch of grass?"

"What else would he see?"

"What wouldn't he see?" Eugene raised his right eyebrow.

These people were driving me crazy. "What are you talking about? You and Harvey and Phil, I don't get you guys. You open your eyes and you see what you see. You have no control over what your eyes see. Please Eugene, just give me the answer so I don't have to hang out with Phil anymore. I can't handle the conversations, the cleaning, and the smell." I was begging Eugene now. "Come on, help me out here. Just tell me. Please. I can't handle the smell."

"I had to clean golf balls with Phil for three months before I figured out what Harvey was talking about," Eugene said with a smile. "Besides, if I told you, Harvey would know you were lying. I'll give you a hint though, the answer's in the bucket," then he took off in the golf cart to go find Harvey.

These people were crazy. There's no answer in a bucket. The only thing in the bucket is a bunch of dirty golf balls.

CHAPTER FIVE

GLASSES

"Let me have your glasses," said Mark Brotherton as he towered over some poor kid while Tommy Rigo bounced around him anxiously.

"I'm not really comfortable giving you my glasses."

"C'mon, give Mark your glasses." Tommy said, in a high-pitched voice.

"I'm not going to do anything to them. I just want to try them on," Mark smirked.

"Yeah, he just wants to try them on." Tommy narrowed his eyes.

"Please guys, just let me get to class."

Mark was becoming a little louder now, "I'll let you go to class after you give me your glasses."

"You're not going anywhere until he gets to wear your glasses." Tommy put his hand on the kid's chest.

This was a scene I'd witnessed many times before. Mark and Tommy were tormenting some poor kid. Probably every school has a Mark and Tommy. Mark was the school bully and Tommy was his evil sidekick. Together, they had the IQ of celery, but that didn't stop them from doing whatever they wanted to whomever they wanted. They were the biggest set of jerks you could ever have the misfortune of meeting.

Mark was by far the largest kid in school. Not large like me, with a flabby gut, but large like a bear that lifted weights and had a personal trainer. The rumor is that Mark flunked at least one grade. No one knew for sure how old he was, but I once saw him shaving in the bathroom. Mark was almost twice as big as the second biggest seventh grader. I had to tolerate Mark because he was one of the best football players on our team, and therefore friends with Calvin, and therefore part of the popular crowd. Mark made me uncomfortable. He scared me. He scared everyone. And you could tell that he liked that power. If you challenged him, he'd turn all his meanness on you. I did my best to stay out of Mark's way.

Mark was usually in trouble one way or another, but he never seemed to care. He got off easier than he should have, because I think most of the teachers were as afraid of him as the rest of us kids. Plus, his mom was the mayor. He was always bragging about it, about how all these important people were coming over to his house. I think his mom would lose the next election in a second if her opponent showed everyone what a jerk her son was.

Tommy was one of the smallest guys in school. He was like Mark's pet. I was surprised that Mark didn't buy Tommy a leash and feed him treats when he was a good boy. Tommy was really hyper. He didn't walk, he bounced. He had these wild, shifty eyes and you could never tell what he was going to do next. Probably the smartest thing that Tommy ever did (maybe the only smart thing he ever did), was to become friends with Mark. Tommy was weird and little and funny looking. He was easily the kind of kid that would get picked on, but because he was friends with Mark, everyone left him alone.

So anyway, there were Mark and Tommy trying to take the glasses from their unfortunate victim. Usually, I just tried to look away when I saw them doing something like that. I knew that it was best not to get involved, or I'd become the next victim. But I couldn't help looking today, because this time the victim was Eugene.

I could tell that Eugene was scared, but he was trying his best to act composed. "Look guys," said Eugene. "I just want to get to earth science. Shouldn't I be able to do that without having to give someone my glasses?"

"Not if I ask you for your glasses, you shouldn't," said Mark.

"Yeah," chimed in Tommy. "Not if Mark asks you for your glasses you shouldn't."

"So what's it gonna be, Eugene? Are you gonna give me your glasses or am I gonna have to take 'em off your face?"

"C'mon guys, just let me go to class." Eugene was pleading with them now.

"What are you gonna do, Eugene? Just give Mark your glasses," Tommy said as he bounced around Eugene.

Eugene put his hands up to his face like he was about

41

to take off his glasses, but then he surprised me—and probably Mark and Tommy even more—he took off running.

Mark and Tommy looked confused for a second. But as dumb as they were, they reacted pretty fast. "Get him!" screamed Mark as they took off after him.

Tommy's a fast runner, and he caught up with Eugene after a few feet. He jumped on his back, but because he's so small, Eugene kept running. He was slowed down with Tommy on his back, and Mark caught up to the two of them. Mark stuck out his foot and tripped Eugene. He fell hard with Tommy on his back. Mark stood over Eugene and helped Tommy to his feet.

"Hey, Eugene, you don't run from me." Mark was furious.

"Yeah," said Tommy between breathes. "You don't run from Mark."

"Now," said Mark, "give me your glasses."

Eugene had no choice this time. He handed his glasses to Mark.

"This will teach you to run from me," said Mark as he snapped Eugene's glasses in half. The boys were directly in front of the girls' bathroom, and Mark saw an opportunity to further humiliate Eugene. Mark opened the door and threw in Eugene's mangled glasses. "Go get 'em, sissy," said Mark and he pushed Eugene into the bathroom, shutting the door behind him.

"Yeah, you big sissy," echoed Tommy, laughing hysterically.

The two of them walked away and Eugene made his

way out of the bathroom. He looked right at me when he made his exit into the hallway. I don't think he could tell it was me though, because his vision was so bad without his glasses.

Sally McCoy came out of the bathroom a moment later. She was holding Eugene's broken glasses. "Are these yours? Someone threw them in here." Sally was trying to be nice, but a few of the popular girls made their way out of the bathroom at the same time, laughing and pointing at Eugene. I didn't understand what was so funny or why people were so mean, but instead of trying to figure it out, I hid behind the door to my locker, avoiding Eugene's glance.

Eugene held out his hand and said, "Yes, they're mine, thanks," and then took the broken pieces from Sally. Eugene stood up and walked quickly down the hall, trying to escape the embarrassment. He was doing a pretty good job of holding it together, but I noticed a tear rolling down his cheek as he walked by.

I couldn't help but think that maybe I could have done something to try to stop that whole thing from happening. I certainly could have done more than just stand there.

I didn't see Eugene again until I went back to work on Saturday. As usual, he was working behind the counter. I noticed right away that he was wearing different glasses. They were a thick black pair, the kind that all the NASA scientists wore in the movie we saw in science class about going to the moon. All the engineers looked exactly the same. They had short hair, wore white button-up shirts with black ties and had a whole bunch of pens in their front shirt pockets. And they all wore the same glasses, like the ones Eugene was wearing now.

Did NASA make everyone who worked there shop at the same store?

Eugene's glasses made him look like he was from the 1960s. I figured that they were probably pretty old. I thought about Eugene having to explain to his parents why his glasses were broken. He either had to lie to them or make up a story. I felt bad for him, and again I felt sorry that I didn't do anything to try to stop Mark and Tommy.

Standing in front of the counter with Eugene across from me, I hung up a sign about some inclement weather expected later that day. We always let golfers know if rain was in the forecast before they went out and played. Eugene was pretty quiet and I thought for sure that he had seen me watch him get attacked by Mark and not do anything. I didn't want to confess though, because maybe he really hadn't seen me. So I just avoided the topic.

"How's it going Eugene?" I asked.

"Pretty good," said Eugene. "Hey, do you want to see a sample of my new grass for the green? Harvey and I have been working on it for a few weeks and it's all grown in now."

"Sure," I said.

Eugene picked up a small plastic container from behind the counter. The bottom of the container was black, and the top was a clear plastic triangle. It looked like a miniature greenhouse. "I've gotten the grass to grow the way I like it to in the greenhouse, but I'm having some problems in real-world weather conditions. Here, feel it." Eugene took the top off the greenhouse and handed the bottom to me. I touched the green sample. It felt like a very thin, densely packed carpet, kind of like my hair. I was impressed.

"Wow, Eugene, that's pretty cool. You designed this whole thing yourself?"

"Well, Harvey helps me a lot. Now, here's the extra surprise…Smell it."

I put my nose to the grass and took a whiff. It didn't smell like a regular lawn, it smelled lemony.

"It's lemon scented," said Eugene. "It's not too strong, just a few lemon tones, but it's there. I went to a lemon orchard when I was two years old. It's my first memory. I remember how good it smelled and how happy it made me. If I could get people to have the same feeling on the green, I bet they'd have more fun golfing." Eugene looked up to the ceiling and smiled. He seemed to be acting the same as he always did, maybe even a little more cheerful than usual. I figured this was a good sign. There was no way he'd be acting so nice to me if he knew that I'd seen what Mark and Tommy did to him and that I hadn't come to help him out. I felt a sense of relief wash over me. I didn't want to hurt his feelings, I was starting to really like Eugene.

I asked him what was on the agenda, and, as usual, he said that Harvey told him I was supposed to go help Phil clean golf balls. Even though I was expecting that, I couldn't help feeling more dread than usual. For the past three weeks, at the end of each shift, I walked away thinking that there was no possible way that Phil could get any weirder, but he always surprised me.

When I sat down next to Phil and began to scrub golf

balls for like the fiftieth day in a row, I was pretty frustrated. But when he got into his crazy cardboard theory, I'd about had it. You see, for a while now, Phil has been formulating this theory about cardboard. According to Phil, cardboard doesn't really exist. During the Truman administration, the president met with space aliens. To quote Phil directly, "The aliens were impressed with our cardboard technology. Despite their superior intelligence and scientific prowess, they were unable to formulate a cardboard of their own." Phil would look up from the golf ball he was cleaning and stare at me whenever he was making an important point, "This was a problem for the aliens because they were moving all the time. Imagine moving without a cardboard box, and you can understand how excited the aliens were when they saw all our cardboard technology.

"So the aliens met with President Harry Truman. To be inconspicuous, they all met at a Motel just outside of Atlantic City, New Jersey. And they asked him for our cardboard formula. But you know, Jason, Truman was no pushover. Harry looked the lead alien in the eye—these aliens only have one eye you know—and said, 'I'm not going to give up all the cardboard in the universe without getting something in return.'

"Now the aliens were friendly, and they really wanted that cardboard, so they pulled out all of their aces. They told Truman that they'd trade their secrets of mind control and object manipulation, or telekinesis, for complete access to our cardboard for all time.

"Good old Harry agreed to the deal. The aliens got all our cardboard, and we got the mind control and object manipulation. Do you know what that means Jason?"

"No." You had to answer Phil. That was one of the worst parts about his stories and theories. You had to be paying attention. If you didn't answer or answered wrong, he'd get all frustrated and explain it again from the beginning, only with much more detail and it would take a lot longer. Phil should have made a career out of interrogation instead of golf ball cleaning. All you had to do was put Phil in a room with someone, and they'd confess to anything to shut him up.

"It means," Phil went on, "that cardboard does not exist on this planet. There's not a scrap of cardboard from here to Siberia. But you have to remember, Jason, what did the aliens give us?"

"Mind control and object manipulation," I unwillingly answered.

"That's right. So the government started using the technology the aliens gave us right away. Through AM radio waves, they broadcast instructions to every man, woman, and child on the planet how to manipulate objects and keep them together, as if the objects are in a cardboard box. So Jason, when you put something into a cardboard box, you're really unwittingly holding it in the air with your mind. Unbelievable, huh?"

"That's amazing," I said in a monotone voice.

Phil smiled wildly, "Outer space, man. Outer space."

There was a moment of silence after Phil's speech and I continued cleaning golf balls, pretending to be deep in thought about cardboard and mind control. I sat there, glad that Phil had finally quit talking. Then, "Hot potatoes!" Phil broke the silence. "We're down to just one bucket of golf balls to clean. Jason, I need you to go to the back nine and look in the deep rough for lost balls. If you do a good job, I'll let you drive the ball-retrieving car on the driving range."

"I'm on my way," I said, running out of the clubhouse before Phil could say another word. It was raining outside, but it didn't bother me. I'd stand out in a monsoon if it meant not having to listen to Phil.

CHAPTER SIX

PLAYING GOLF

I walked out to hole ten, happily following Phil's instructions. Just by hanging around a golf course and being around Eugene, I was learning a little bit about the game. Plus I had taken a book out of our school library and started reading a little about it too. I thought that maybe if I learned more about golf by studying the game enough, eventually I would be able to answer Harvey's question correctly and would never be stuck cleaning balls with Phil again.

Here's a little bit of what I learned during that first month of working at Whispering Canyon. On our course there are eighteen holes. Most golf courses have eighteen holes. Some have nine, though. According to Eugene, nine-hole courses are called executive courses. Don't ask me why. Executive courses are for beginners or players that are simply trying to work on their short game, which means hitting shots from inside one hundred yards or so. On an eighteen-hole course, even though the holes go in order, they are split up between the front nine and the back nine. The front nine consists of holes one through nine, and the back nine are holes ten through eighteen. Hole nine is located by the clubhouse. You go away from the clubhouse when you take your first shot and sort of work your way back to the clubhouse when you get to hole nine. You do the same at hole ten. You go away from the clubhouse and work your way back, so that by the time you're done at hole eighteen, you're back at the clubhouse, which is where everyone parks their cars and buys hot dogs or turkey sandwiches.

When you finish the first nine holes and start up again at hole ten, this is called making the turn. Eugene says that splitting the course into two halves is a good thing because it gives golfers a fresh start. This is kind of like halftime in a football or a basketball game.

When playing a hole of golf, you start (or tee off), from the tee box. There are three places to tee off from. The farthest place from the hole is where the experts tee off. Regular people tee off from the middle box, and women and beginners tee off from closest to the hole. I told Eugene that it wasn't fair that women got things easier than men, but Eugene insisted that, "It's a biological fact that most men are stronger than most women. It doesn't mean that they're worse golfers than men, on average they just don't hit the ball as far as men do. It doesn't make things easier for women, it levels the playing field." I could tell that Eugene had thought about this subject before, and by the time he had finished his explanation I was in complete agreement with him.

The drive, which is your first shot off the tee, should be your longest shot of the hole. The goal is to hit the ball as far as you can away from the tee box and as close to the hole as possible, while keeping the ball straight and on the fairway. When you tee off, you usually use big clubs called woods, even though they're made out of metal. Eugene says that they used to be made out of wood, and the name just stuck. It's a little confusing if you ask me. You put the golf ball on this wooden or plastic thing called a tee. Eugene says that having the ball off the ground means that you can really knock the snot out of it. Those are my words not his, but I think that you understand my point.

When you hit from the tee, you want the ball to land in the fairway. The book I read went into great detail about how the grass on the fairway is cut pretty short, so it's easy to hit the ball, rewarding you for an accurate tee shot. But if you screw up off the tee and the ball doesn't land in the fairway, it's called hitting into the rough. The rough is not mowed as closely as the fairway, so the ball's harder to hit. If you really screw up and hit the ball deep into the woods, this is called hitting it into the deep rough. They don't mow the grass in the deep rough at all, so *if* you find your ball, it's really hard to hit. Eugene told me that even if your ball lands in a tree, you have to play it from the tree. According to Eugene, most golfers take what's called a penalty stroke, rather than go find their golf ball deep in the woods.

A penalty stroke is adding one stroke to your final score on the hole. So if you got the ball in the cup, which Eugene sometimes calls it instead of the pin, in four strokes, but you got a penalty stroke, your score would actually be a five. I think the same thing happens if you hit the ball into the water, but you might get two strokes added on or something. I can't remember.

That's the thing about golf. Before I started working at Whispering Canyon, I thought golf was the least complicated sport in the world. I mean, you hit a ball with a stick, walk after it, and then hit it again until you get it in the hole. Plus, I played miniature golf, and that's pretty easy to understand. I thought golf would be the same. But the more Eugene told me, and the more I read about it in my book, the more I understood that it's pretty complicated. There are all these weird rules; there are even ways you're supposed to behave when you're playing. Like if you're playing slow and someone behind you catches up, you're supposed to let them go ahead of you so they don't have to wait. I'm not trying to say that I love golf or anything, it's just not as completely boring and stupid as I thought it was before I was forced to work here. Plus, I like the fact that you have to wear a collared shirt on a golf course. What other sport could I play in my suit?

Anyway, since lots of golfers either take a penalty stroke or can't find their golf ball when they hit it into the deep rough, there are lots of golf balls hiding in the woods. This is really exciting to Phil. The golf balls you find in the deep rough are often muddy. Phil takes it as a personal challenge to get an impossibly dirty golf ball clean. He has a secret cleaning solution he made up just for cleaning extra-dirty golf balls. He told me about it, but he won't let me see it. He saves the dirtiest golf balls for days that I don't work. Phil told me that he's going to market his cleaning solution once he patents it and that he'll make millions of dollars. Then he's finally going to publish his book about the whole mind-control-cardboard-alien-Truman thing. Lookout best-seller list, here comes Phil.

So there I was, standing in the deep rough on hole ten, looking for lost balls. Finding golf balls in the deep rough got me away from Phil, so I was more than happy to do it. After I was done with holes ten, eleven, and twelve, I made my way to hole thirteen. By then, I probably had about fifty golf balls in my bucket.

Hole thirteen was a pretty cool hole because there was a huge pond right next to the fairway. If you screwed up on hole thirteen, you lost your golf ball in the pond and got a penalty no matter what, unless you wanted to play your ball from underwater. This was the hole where golfers get the angriest. They cursed and sometimes threw a club into the pond. In the summer, Eugene gets to go snorkeling in the pond to retrieve all the good stuff. Harvey said that maybe next summer I could help him out. Besides loads of golf balls, he told me that in just one summer he found ten golf clubs, three golf bags, nine golf shoes, four hats, and my favorite, a pair of pants. How mad would someone have to get to take their pants off and throw them into a pond? Did they play the rest of the game in their underwear? I pictured some guy going home and having to explain to his wife why he came back from the golf course without his pants. That always made me laugh.

I went to the edge of the pond to see if I could find anything good. And sure enough, right there at my feet was a golf club. I reached down and picked it up. It was still shiny and didn't look like it had been there too long. There was a big number five on the bottom of the club head, which indicated that my first golf club was a five iron.

Even though I had been working at a golf course for close to a month, besides that day with my dad when I was seven, this was the first time that I'd ever held a golf club in my hands. I'd seen people swing a club on TV, and I'd seen plenty of them swing since I'd been working here, so I just pretended like I was one of them. I started swinging it around. I figured since I had so many golf balls with me, it would be fun to hit a couple of them into the pond. Just a few. I knew Phil was nuts, but I didn't think he was nuts enough to notice a few missing golf balls.

I walked back into the middle of the fairway and put a ball down in front of me. I took a few steps back, ran, and swung at the ball. Instead of hitting the ball, I launched a big chunk of grass into the air. I didn't even come close to hitting it. I ran and got the clump of grass and tried to put it back as best I could. Maybe I shouldn't try to hit the ball while running, I thought.

I tried again, this time with my feet planted firmly on the ground, shifting my body weight by twisting my waist with the motion of the club. I brought the club back as fast as I could, then swung as hard and as fast as possible. I didn't hit any grass on this one, but I also didn't hit the ball. All I did was hit the air. Maybe I should slow down my swing, I thought to myself. So I brought the club back slowly, and slowly, I went for the ball.

I hit it this time, but it didn't go very far, just a few feet in front of me. Still, I was excited that I had hit it at all. I walked up to the ball and tried again, this time bending my knees so that I would get under the ball more. Boom! I crushed one and stood in shock as I watched it sail through the air and land in the water with a satisfying splash. I laughed out loud. I can't really explain why hitting a little round ball into a pond was so fun, but it was. I was playing golf and to my surprise, I liked it.

So I got out another ball and tried again. The ball went over the pond this time. I tried another, then another, then another. Some of the balls went into the pond, some went a few feet in front of me, some went to the left or right, some I missed completely, and one somehow went behind me.

Then, from out of nowhere, a voice startled me, "Your swing's off a little."

I turned around. It was Harvey. Because it was raining, he was wearing a yellow rubber rain jacket. His beard poked out of it and made him look like a soggy teddy bear.

"Uh, hi, Harvey," I said. "How long have you been here?"

"Long enough to see you hit all of Phil's golf balls into the water hazard, and long enough to see that your swing needs lots of work. Of course, I could see that from just one swing. Was that the first time you ever swung a golf club?"

"I've done it once before when I was seven," I said. I was praying not to get in trouble. If Harvey fired me, I swear my parent's would send me to military school. But he just kept going and didn't seem mad at all.

"You did pretty well for your first time. Did you like it?"

This was a strange conversation, but I wasn't going to be the one bringing up the fact that I was supposed to be getting into trouble, so I just went along with Harvey. "Yes," I answered definitively. "I did like it." In fact, I liked it more than most other things that I'd tried in my life. "It felt great when the ball went where I wanted it to go."

"Good. I think you have some natural ability, Jason. Would you like to learn more?"

"Okay," I said. If I said yes, maybe Harvey wouldn't get me in trouble.

"Well, here's your first lesson. After your shift on Sunday, I want you to spend two hours watching people tee off from hole one."

"That's it?" I asked.

"That's it," said Harvey. "I want you to watch how people swing the club. Make a note to yourself and see what people do when they hit the ball well and pay attention to what people do when they hit the ball poorly. You can report back to me on Sunday."

"Sounds good." It looked like I was going to get away with this after all.

"Oh, Jason, one more thing…" Harvey walked to his golf cart and got out a weird-looking golf club. He handed it to me. It was this crazy-looking thing. Instead of a club head, it had a circular ring on top. "This is a ball retriever," said Harvey. "You use it to get golf balls out of water. I'd like you to retrieve all of Phil's golf balls that you hit into the water hazard. I'd recommend the ball retriever, but if you're really in a hurry, feel free to take a dip in the pond. I'll see you on Sunday."

Harvey laughed and got into his golf cart and drove away. I guess I got what was coming to me. Still, I couldn't help feel excited about learning more about golf.

CHAPTER SEVEN

MY FIRST LESSON

I finished my shift on Sunday without incident. Phil didn't go nuts about me hitting his precious golf balls into the pond, so I guessed that Harvey hadn't mention anything to him.

Before I walked over to the first tee box to spy on golfers, I had to listen to Phil explain how the platypus is actually a pet to alien children. According to Phil, "When the aliens were on a collecting trip in Australia, one of the little Shu aliens brought a pair of pet platypuses," Phil says that there aren't male and female aliens, there are five kinds: Shu, Sha, Shem, Shrem, and Bev. Shu are the young aliens, then they eventually turn into one of the other four kinds. The platypuses got loose, and without many predators, they spread like wildfire. "I mean, think about it Jason, what other animal has fur, lays eggs, has a bill, and lactates through its fur?" He didn't even wait for me to answer, "I'll tell you, no other kind of animal.

It's so completely obvious that platypuses are not of this world. Anyone who tells you otherwise is probably an alien himself. I'm writing a book about it." Phil continued scrubbing a golf ball and I left him for the day.

I guess listening to this story was better then getting in trouble with Phil. I can't imagine what he would have done if he found out how poorly I treated his golf balls. He'd probably write another book about it. Either way, I was glad when my shift was over.

I went to the tee box of hole one after my shift to begin my first golf lesson. Harvey had told me to watch people and see what they did when they hit the ball well and what they did when they hit the ball poorly. I was actually looking forward to this. It was a sunny afternoon for a change, and it felt nice to be outside. I took off my sport coat and grabbed a seat about twenty yards back from the tee, sort of hidden behind a small tree. I didn't want to draw attention to myself while spying on these golfers.

Since it was such a nice day, the golf course was packed. There were lots of people around. Harvey was out telling groups when it was their turn to tee off. Everyone had to be in a group of four on the crowded days. Sometimes a group of four would sign up together, and other times, two single golfers would be placed with a pair of other golfers. Or two pairs would form a foursome. Or a single would join a group of three. Or four singles would form a foursome. I'm pretty sure that's all the combinations of golfers that you can get with a foursome.

The first foursome was the combination of two very different couples. I assumed that they were both married. I got the impression that the couples didn't know each other. Both pairs looked a little older than my parents. I named one of the couples The Twins because they were both wearing the exact same clothing. They even looked alike. Both had dark hair, both were trim, and both were groomed neatly. The other couple I called the Pair of Pain because they looked so upset. They hadn't even teed off yet and they already looked like they'd just lost the World Series or something. The man had an angry red face and red sunburn on his chest that was exposed because the top two buttons of his shirt were opened. The angry woman, his wife I guessed, didn't look any more comfortable.

The Twins introduced themselves to the Pair of Pain. Mr. Twin extended his hand to Mr. Pain, "Hello," he said, "my name is Stanley McFeely. This is my wife Shirley. Beautiful day for a round of golf, don't you think?"

Mr. Pain shook Mr. McFeely's hand as if he was shaking hands with a snake. "I'm Martin Sanders," he mumbled, abruptly. "It would be a nice day for golf if my wife, Helen, hadn't forgotten her golf shoes." Mr. Sanders pointed an angry finger at Mrs. Sanders's feet. She was wearing regular shoes. I didn't see why Mrs. Sanders forgetting her golf shoes would upset her husband so much, but clearly it did. Mrs. Sanders just stared blankly ahead, pretending she couldn't hear people talking about her four feet away.

"Well, would you like the honors?" Mr. McFeely asked Mr. Sanders with a smile.

"No," said Mr. Sanders sharply. "I never, ever tee off first. Never."

"Very well then," said Mr. McFeely, clearly trying to

make the best of the situation after realizing he had been paired up with the two angriest people on the planet. "Honey, would you like to go first?"

"I'd love to," said Mrs. McFeely.

"Go get 'em," Mr. McFeely cheered his wife on, sporting another huge smile.

Mrs. McFeely took out her driver and went to the tee box. She pulled a tee out of her pocket and sunk it into the ground about halfway. Eugene tried to tell me why having the ball raised is a good thing, but he started to get into some pretty complicated physics, explaining that because the golf ball is off the ground you actually want to hit the ball when your swing is going down. Also, according to Eugene, the driver is one of the hardest clubs to hit well because it's the longest club, and therefore you stand further away from the ball than if you were using another club. This creates more leverage, allowing you to hit the ball farther, but it's also harder to control. All this doesn't make much sense to me. Still, I admired Eugene for his passion. I don't think I've ever felt that strongly about anything, let alone a sport. But I have to admit Eugene's love for golf was a little contagious.

I'm getting off track, though. I'm supposed to be watching golf here. I'm supposed to be watching Mrs. McFeely tee off. So after she placed a golf ball on the top of the tee she had wedged into the ground, she took two practice swings, calmly approaching her golf ball after she was finished. She then lined her club up with the ball, took a deep breath, looked down the fairway, and then looked back at the ball one last time. Then she swung. The best way for me to describe her swing was smooth. Her body swiveled with her club, moving back when the club was back and then forward as she swung through the ball. There was a distinct "ping" that sounded as her club made contact with the ball. Harvey had once said that when you became a real golfer, you could hear good shots. I was starting to see what he meant. Sure enough, the ball flew in a straight line and landed right in the middle of the fairway.

"Nice shot, honey," said Mr. McFeely.

"Thank you," replied Mrs. McFeely. "I guess you're up now."

Mr. McFeely took out his driver and placed a tee in the white tee box. He set his ball down on top of the tee. Like Mrs. McFeely, he stepped back, but he only took one practice swing. He then moved up next to the ball, looked down the fairway, looked at the ball, and swung. His ball also flew in a straight line. It landed right in the middle of the fairway, only Mr. McFeely's shot went a lot farther than Mrs. McFeely's.

"Great shot, honey," said Mrs. McFeely.

"Thank you," replied Mr. McFeely. He turned to the Sanders. "So, who's up next?"

Mr. Sanders looked at Mr. McFeely like he was asking the world's hardest question. "Me," he said sharply.

Although the McFeelys were calm and cool when they approached the tee box, Mr. Sanders was nervous and quick. He teed up his ball in the same spot that Mr. McFeely hit from. But unlike Mr. and Mrs. McFeely, he took about seven or eight practice swings. I noticed that he swung the club much faster than the McFeelys. He was a bundle of angry energy. Now, I didn't know much about golf, but I knew that based on his practice swings that his shot wasn't going to be a good one.

Mr. Sanders turned to the McFeelys, "Don't watch me when I swing. I hate it when people watch me swing." The McFeelys turned their heads slightly, with a look of surprise on both of their faces.

Sanders stepped up to the ball and took a gigantic swing. He must have done something wrong, though, because he barely even hit the ball. There was a loud thud, nothing like the ping I'd heard when The Twins hit. The ball bounced a few times in front of him and landed about twenty feet past the womens' tee box.

"This club stinks," he shouted, tossing his driver toward his golf bag.

"Way to go, Martin. Beautiful shot," said Mrs. Sanders sarcastically.

"I'd like to see you do better," snapped Mr. Sanders, with his face turning a deeper shade of red. I felt sorry that the McFeelys had to spend seventeen more holes with him, and even sorrier that Mrs. Sanders had to spend the rest of her life with him.

"Maybe I will," said Mrs. Sanders.

She walked up to the womens' tee box. Like everyone else, she put the ball down on top of the tee. She looked down the fairway once, then swung. She didn't take a practice swing. I guess she didn't need to. She hit a beautiful shot that landed in between Mr. and Mrs. McFeely's shots. She shot her husband a snide glance. "Huh, just think of how well I would have done if I had my golf shoes," said Mrs. Sanders.

Mr. Sanders looked like he was going to explode. I've

never seen someone get so red. He looked like a tomato.

I spent a few more hours at the first tee. I thought it would be boring, but it turned out to be fun. After watching nine or ten foursomes, I was able to identify some patterns. I started making predictions about each person's shot based on what they did before they hit the ball. It was pretty cool, almost like a science project. And for the most part, I was pretty right on.

Here are the conclusions I made: Overall, people who looked relaxed did much better than people who looked nervous. Taking lots of practice swings doesn't help you. The faster you swing the club, the more likely you are to hit a bad shot. Losing your balance almost always means a bad shot. Golf pants are funny looking. People who looked up early to watch their ball usually didn't hit the ball very far. If you looked angry or distracted, you were going to hit a bad shot.

At the end of the day I was pretty tired. I made my way into the pro shop where Harvey was waiting for me. Without hesitation he asked me a question that got right to the heart of the issue. "What did you learn?"

"I learned a lot, Harvey." I stopped for a second, thinking about the right answer to his question, the answer that would free me from Phil and his alien theories. "The grip," I started, but then stopped. That wasn't what he wanted. "You have to point your feet," again I stopped, taking a deep breath. "You see, the practice swing," when I stopped this time I closed my eyes for a moment and thought deeply. What did you learn? Harvey's question echoed inside of my head. A moment later,

I opened my eyes. I knew the answer.

It wasn't about seeing the game the way I watched it on television. I wasn't supposed to report on all the details. I started speaking from my heart, "Golf's not only played on the course. It's played in your head." I started to speak with more confidence, "The way I see it, is that everyone has this great swing inside of them, it hides though. You have to feel the shot in order to hit the ball and make it go where you want. Seeing the shot in your head helps you bring the shot out of your body. But you have to be calm and cool. Golf's not at all about stepping up to the ball and just hitting it. The state of mind you're in is everything."

When I finished talking, I couldn't believe what had just come out of my mouth. Had I really learned all that? I glanced up at Harvey and saw a new look in his eyes. For the first time ever, I was talking about golf and he was nodding in approval. "Well, you're ready to start playing, so that's good." This comment made me smile as we walked over to the first tee together. When we stood facing down the fairway, Harvey followed up his first question, by asking me the question he had been posing every time I saw him for an entire month. "What do you see in front of you on the way to the green?"

I shrugged my shoulders, a little disappointed. Although I'd made strides that day in understanding golf, I still didn't know the answer.

CHAPTER EIGHT

THE REAL JASON GREEN

The first few weeks at Whispering Canyon had been pretty torturous, as I spent every afternoon cleaning golf balls with Phil. But after my first lesson, Harvey, Eugene, and I started playing together a few times a week after our shift was over. I actually started to look forward to heading to work each day. That, and my new physical conditioning, had completely changed my life.

It was hard to believe that I'd been working at Whispering Canyon for nearly three months. The great thing was that during this time period I'd actually gotten good at golf. I was consistently shooting in the mid nineties, which was a really good score for a thirteen-year-old kid. And I was enjoying myself too. I even went out with Mom and Dad one day. They were so excited by the way I was playing they told me that my punishment was officially over. I'd already paid for the damages on the Flight to Mars and I'd sent a beautiful flower arrangement to the girls that I scared. Mom said that I could have my weekends back if I wanted to. But to my surprise, I didn't want them back. I'd fallen in love with playing golf and knew that the only way I'd be able to play all the time was by keeping my job. Plus, it was fun working with Harvey and Eugene.

I did stay at Whispering Canyon. And as the weeks passed, with the practice I was getting in, my new weight-training regimen, and the tips I continued to get from Harvey, I continually improved my game. Dad even started talking about me joining the golf team when I got to high school. He was thinking scholarship all the way. Even Phil commented on how fast I was learning and what a natural I was. He started to tell me about the aliens and how they were natural golfers. Then he'd look at me strangely. (I was sure Phil was convinced that I was an alien too, but he never mentioned anything.) I couldn't really believe it myself, but playing golf just felt right. Something about the game clicked with me and I'd become a golfer.

Still, always getting Harvey's question wrong made me feel like I was missing some key piece about the game, and it really bothered me. So I'd been doing a lot of thinking about what I'd been learning, and what Eugene said about the answer being at the bottom of the bucket. I understood golf much better then I did when I began working at Whispering Canyon, so this time when Harvey asked me the question, I was sure I knew the answer.

"What do you see in front of you, Jason?" Harvey asked.

I answered with confidence, "I see a spot in the middle of the fairway about a hundred and eighty yards from here. I see the ball bouncing twice and rolling to a stop right there."

Harvey looked and me and smiled. "Good. You've learned the lesson that can't be taught, Jason."

"Finally," I muttered, halfway smiling.

"Learning to focus is something you needed to discover yourself. Now that you know this skill, there is no limit to where you can go—with your golf game and in life."

I was excited that I'd finally gotten the question right. I really had been thinking a lot about all that Harvey was teaching me. He was always trying to get me to clear my head before a shot, "Take aim and fire, let your body do the thinking about the shot, not your brain." So when Harvey posed his question again, I kept thinking about what someone who cleared his head and let his body do the thinking would see before he took a shot. It made sense to me that all he would see is what he was aiming for. Everything else would fade away. It's like looking into the bottom of an empty bucket. All you saw was the end.

It was weird. Nothing like this had ever happened to me before. I was exercising every day, I could see my toes in the shower, I cared about what I ate, my pants were falling down, and it was all because of golf. The most boring and slow sport in the universe was getting me into shape. I didn't even mean for it to happen, but I guess it makes sense.

I used to think that walking up and down the stairs was exercise, I got excited when I played video games, and I always figured that gave me plenty of energy. Turns out I was wrong. I was way out of shape. When I first started at Whispering Canyon I couldn't even walk the front nine. Swinging a club ten times made me tired. But after working at Whispering Canyon, I could easily walk the whole course while carrying a full bag of clubs. Sometimes I even carried Harvey's bag, too. I'd be out on the course practicing for hours without even realizing it. So far I had even lost over thirty pounds.

I was also lifting weights. We had this old machine called a Superflexer that lived in our garage. It's a weight training station, but instead of weights it uses thick rubber bands. The more rubber bands you put on, the harder it is to do an exercise. My dad ordered the machine when I was six, but I had never seen anyone use it. The only time anyone ever went near it was when my parents had a big dinner party and hung peoples' coats on it.

You might be wondering why someone playing golf needs to lift weights. I used to think that the only purpose of lifting weights was to look good and to be able to beat up on people who can't lift as much weight. That's why football players did it, right? But I was at the library researching my report on rodents for science class and was looking up some stuff about gophers when I came across some more golf books. I couldn't believe how many there were. There were books about presidents who golfed. There were books on putting. There were books on the long game, the short game, and on designing a golf course. There was even a book all about the history of the golf ball.

So I pulled a few books off the shelf and read about the game. It was really cool. Here are some of the most interesting facts I pulled out of my reading: Golf has been around for over

500 years, making it one of the world's oldest sports. Many people think it started with shepherds in Scotland. You may never have more than fourteen golf clubs in your golf bag. The very first golf balls were called featheries. They were called that because they were made out a bunch of leather strips sewn together and stuffed with feathers. Someone who cheats in golf is called a sandbagger.

I was reading about the history of the game and I got into a section called "Conditioning for Golf." According to the author, "The purpose of weight conditioning for golf is not to build excessive muscle mass but to increase flexibility and muscle balance. The increased flexibility and balance gained from exercise gives a conditioned golfer a biomechanical edge over a golfer who does not weight train." A bio-mechanical edge? I didn't know what that was, but I wanted one.

So I made a xerox copy of the exercises I was supposed to do and brought them home. I could modify most of them so that I could do them on the Superflexer. Early on, I could barely do any of the exercises, and after my first day of weight conditioning, I was so sore that I couldn't lift my hands above my shoulders. But I kept at it, and after a few weeks, the soreness went away. It actually felt good. I really was getting more flexible, too. But the best part was that the exercising seemed to improve my game. I could drive farther than ever before. Even Harvey commented on it.

Eugene was also excited about my drives. I told him about lifting weights and he wanted to join me. So we started lifting together. Eugene would come over on Tuesdays and Thursdays (days we weren't working) and after work on Saturday. We were about the funniest weight-lifting pair that you could ever hope to see. Eugene was skinny, tall, and wore bad glasses, whereas I was short and not at all athletic looking. We looked like the before in those before-and-after pictures of miracle muscle-building shakes that you can order from late-night TV. But we were having fun.

It got to be that Eugene and I were spending lots of time together. I would see him almost every day. If we weren't lifting weights or talking about golf, we found something else fun to do. I'd been over to his house and he had come over to mine. We didn't only talk about golf anymore, we talked about other things like school and movies. Eugene even told me about the crush he had on Sally McCoy. He showed me all the projects he was conducting around the house. They were impressive. In the kitchen, he was inventing a new kind of cheese. He showed me the putting green he made in the backyard with his Eugene Green Grass.

His room was the coolest room I've ever seen. On the ceiling he painted a scale model of the Milky Way. He explained, "It glows at night and makes me feel like I'm outside. It helps me relax and think about things." Little pieces of track ran all over his walls. The tracks branched out across the room and looked like a network of tiny veins. I noticed little trains running on the tracks. "Those are my elevator trains," Eugene told me. He made a robot that folded his clothes and put them away. "It's a simple design, really. The secret is parabolic gears." He had a chameleon colony. "Chameleons are a very difficult species to raise because they're so delicate," he told me. "But they're amazing to watch aren't they?" He was right, they were amazing to watch.

We didn't do the "right" things that I did when I was with Calvin and the cool kids. Instead of hanging out at the mall, we had potato-growing competitions. We would climb trees. We invented a game called The Sock that was played only using pairs of socks. I guess you could say that Eugene and I were becoming pretty good friends. I know that technically the stuff we liked to do made us nerds, but we usually had such a good time together that it didn't really matter.

The only time it mattered was at school. At school it was like Eugene and I weren't friends. It was probably the only thing we never talked about. I would pass him in the halls and sort of say hello to him, but that was it. We never ate lunch together. I stayed at the cool section and Eugene ate quickly by himself and spent most of lunch in the library researching golf course production.

The way the cool kids acted was bothering me more and more. Before I started hanging out with Eugene and playing golf, it never occurred to me to question that there might be something wrong with the whole structure of coolness at school. I always thought the popular kids were popular because they were the coolest kids at school. Everyone else wanted to be like them because being like them was the coolest thing to do.

But compare Eugene with Mark Brotherton and something just didn't match up. Eugene was smart, funny, and thought of cool things to do all the time. Mark was stupid, unfunny, and just thought about being mean all the time. So why was Mark the one that got to go to all the school dances? Why did lots of girls like Mark and no one really like Eugene?

It wasn't fair.

I didn't know what I could do about it. So I did nothing. I mean, how could I possibly change the structure of school popularity? I'm sure even in the old days all kids cared about at school was being popular. Like if someone's mom was the mayor of the town, that kid was probably cool. He'd be invited to all the square dances, while little Thomas Edison was at home, exiled to his room inventing the light bulb.

It was almost like I was living two lives. I had my golf life and then my cool life. The two worlds were totally separate and they felt totally opposite. I was too scared to do anything to rock the boat with the cool kids, though, so I just went along like I was the same old Jason. Only I wasn't. I was changing.

I started to notice things like the way my best friend at school, Calvin, didn't act the way a best friend was supposed to act. He could be so cool one minute, and then he could be almost as bad as Mark Brotherton the next. When Calvin and I were hanging out together, just the two of us, it was great. We'd talk about all kinds of stupid stuff—mostly girls we liked and video games. But when Calvin was with the rest of the cool kids, it's like he was a different person.

Like in history class one day, we had to split up into pairs. Calvin and I usually paired up together, but that day he partnered with Dave Cordura. It made me really mad. I had to join a group with Pete McClean. Working with Pete was a lot like working with Phil. They both smelled a lot and talked a lot about stuff that only they were interested in. And you had to listen to them. So there was me, the chubby class clown with horrible hair and a cheap suit, paired up with Pete McClean, also with horrible hair, horrible clothes, and man, the smell. Pete's stench was almost like another person. We were a threesome, not a pair.

And then there were Calvin and Dave. The cool pair. Calvin, you already know, was as cool as they come. Dave's no stranger to coolness either. His dad owned a bunch of car dealerships, so Dave was always wearing the coolest clothes and listening to the latest music on his portable CD player. And like Calvin, Dave usually had some girl obsessed with him.

Compare Pete and me with Calvin and Dave and it was clear that our groups made perfect sense. The Calvins and the Daves of the world were supposed to be paired up in history groups and teamed up to play sports together. They were supposed to go out to the mall with two other girls who were as popular as they were. And the Jason Greens and Pete McCleans were supposed to be together as well.

You see, the difference between Calvin and me is that when Calvin was at school, he needed to be cool. And he needed to be cool more than he needed to be friends with me. For Calvin, it was cooler to be in a group with super-stud Dave Codura than Jason Green, the joke.

The question was why did I need to be friends with Calvin and his jerky crew? Why was all of this popularity so important to me? Who says that popular is right? And why was I thinking about all of this just because I got partnered up with Pete?

Throughout the rest of that day I couldn't stop thinking

about what happened in history. I knew that on the surface, it probably wasn't a big deal and I'm sure that Calvin didn't even think twice about the whole thing. But ever since I started working at the golf course and hanging out with Eugene and Harvey, somehow something seemed different. I was starting to realize who I really was.

CHAPTER NINE

A DREAM IS BORN

Things at Whispering Canyon were really coming into swing (get it?). As spring approached and the weather improved, more people started coming to the course. Phil could hardly keep up with all the golf balls that needed cleaning. Phil was weird when he wasn't overwhelmed, but when he was, he was downright crazy. He started singing to golf balls that he thought were tired, wrapping golf balls in plastic when it rained (even though he cleaned them indoors), and he even went so far as to bury a few broken golf balls behind the pro shop.

Luckily for me, Harvey needed extra hands out on the course, so I spent most of my time with him and Eugene outside. I usually only had to spend half a day each week with Phil, which was still more than enough, believe me. Phil's latest theory was weird even for Phil. It had something to do with flies and how they were actually evolutions of microscopic alien spacecraft that got stranded on Earth millions of years ago. "They were trying to get home to the mother planet, Jason, but they got confused and just flew around eating each other. Pretty sad, you know?" I'm not sure if I'm getting the whole story right, but I think that you get the picture. Anyway, it was good to be spending as little time as possible with Phil. And it was great to be spending time with Eugene and Harvey.

Before I started working at Whispering Canyon, golf looked so easy and stupid when I watched it on TV. But after playing it for a while, I've gotta confess, it's tough. Some days, for whatever reason, you just can't even hit the ball. It's an unexplainable phenomenon. Imagine playing basketball every day for a year, and then waking up one day and being unable to dribble or even hit the rim on a jumper. That's like golf. Pro golfers call it the "shanks" and Harvey says it has something to do with a player's emotional balance that day. Harvey says that because golf is so mental, it's the hardest game in the world. He explained it to me one day when I was doing poorly and getting frustrated, "Jason, don't allow yourself to get upset. Remember, you're playing the hardest game in the world."

"You think golf is harder than boxing?" I asked.

"Yes, I do."

"Football?"

"Yes."

I thought about it for a minute and tried to think of a sport harder than golf. "I bet dogsled racing is way harder than golf."

"In my experience, there is no game more challenging than golf. In any other game there is a ball moving or an opponent moving, and you are forced to react quickly to that movement. When something is moving quickly, you don't have time to think about what to do. You just do it. But in golf, you have too much time, Jason. You slowly walk up to the ball, which is lying still on the ground; there is no defense, no clock, just you and the ball and time to think about what to do. Naturally, instead of just hitting the ball, your mind gets in the way. That's why great golfers are the ones who can clear their minds and simply take aim and swing. An unlearned golfer is clouded by too much thought. Thoughts of grips and balance and knees, all these thoughts make the swing impure. Plus, there are other thoughts crowding a golfer's brain, thoughts that surface during the restless moments before your swing—nervousness, anxiety, and self-consciousness. These thoughts can do more harm to a swing than using a fishing pole as a club. Do you understand what I'm saying, Jason?"

"I think so. It's kind of like what you were talking about when you made me walk the course that time. If I thought too hard about walking, it was hard, but when I just did it, it was easy."

A small smile spread across Harvey's face and he patted me on the back, "That is precisely right."

Golf made sense to me like that. I liked the way you had to use your brain and think about a shot before you took it. I liked being outside in the fresh air, lost among the trees, the green grass, and the chirping birds. I found that I liked walking and carrying my own clubs too. Driving the golf cart was fun, but I never seemed to play as well as when I walked. Most of all, I liked the feeling I got when I made a good shot. This feeling is especially great because of how difficult the game of golf is. So when the ball lands where you want it to, it makes you feel like you can do anything. Watching that little white dimpled thing fly through the air, and knowing that I was the one who put it there, made me feel great. I don't think I can fully explain it, it's just cool.

I found myself wanting to play all the time. I was always looking for ways to get better and spend more time on the course. When it rained, I'd watch lots of golf on TV and try to learn from what they were doing right and from what mistakes they were making. During work, I'd hang out with Harvey as much as I could. He always had a pointer or some advice for me. For the first time in my life, I felt like I really fit in somewhere and I really cared about something.

I realized this as I was teeing off at the third hole one Saturday after work. Eugene went before me. In golf, it's customary for the person who got the best score to tee off first. This is called taking the honor. When I played with Eugene, he almost always had the honor. Although I might have some natural golf ability, Eugene's been playing since he was three years old, and he really knows the game. He's probably one of the best thirteen-year-olds in the state of Washington. The good thing is that he's never a jerk about being better than me. I can only imagine what it would be like playing a sport with Calvin. I'd probably have to listen to him brag about how great he was the whole time.

So, as usual, Eugene hit a beautiful tee shot that landed right in the middle of the fairway. He probably couldn't have hit a better one. It was near perfect. I followed him, teed up my ball, and took my two practice swings. I stared down the middle of the fairway and pictured hitting the exact same shot as Eugene. I saw the ball landing there before I even hit it. Then I stepped up to the ball and swung away without thinking about anything else.

Something felt right about that swing. I could tell that it was going to be a good shot before I even looked up from my stance. And I was right. The ball was flying in a beautiful arc, not too high and not too low. And it was going right over the fairway. It hit the ground, bounced twice, and landed right next to Eugene's golf ball. It was like the ball knew exactly where I wanted it to go, and it landed there. I smiled with pride as I put my driver back into my bag.

Eugene and I walked over to the fairway to get a closer look at where our golf balls landed. When we approached, we saw the two of them touching one another. There were hundreds of feet of lush grass in every direction, and these two balls had landed within an inch of one another. The two of us stood over the balls, contemplating the odds of this happening.

"Wow, I've never seen that before," said Eugene.

"Yeah, me neither," I said. There was a pause for another few seconds.

"Pretty cool, huh?" Eugene smiled. "At least we're together in the fairway and not a sand trap or something."

"Yeah." He was right. It made me feel really good about my golf game, knowing that I was even with Eugene, even if only for one shot. "So what are we supposed to do when this happens, Eugene? We can't just hit, we'll knock the other person's golf ball off the fairway. You can't do that, can you?"

"No, I don't think so," said Eugene. He looked up at the sky for a second like he always did when he was thinking. "I think there's a rule in golf that if your ball is obstructed by something artificial on the course, you get what's called a drop. You can pick up your ball and drop it one arm's length away from the obstruction, just as long as you don't move the ball closer to the hole."

"But which one of the golf balls is an obstruction?" I asked.

"I guess mine is," Eugene said, "since it was there first. I guess you get the drop."

"Okay," I said.

I picked up the ball and dropped it an arm's length away from Eugene's golf ball. Then I grabbed my five iron and took my customary two practice swings. There was something mystical about the last shot that I had hit, and I felt really great. When I looked toward the green, which was about 155 yards away, I didn't just pick a spot and swing. Instead, I stared directly at the hole. All my focus was on that pin. Then I stepped up to the ball and made my real swing. It was like the shot was in slow motion. When I struck the ball, my club stayed smooth and on course with my body. I followed through completely and watched the ball sail toward the green, climbing higher and higher into the sky and then beginning its descent.

I focused on the ball as it made its way back toward the earth. I heard Eugene over my shoulder. His voice was deep, also in slow motion. "Great shot, Jason." Then I watched the ball hit the center of the green and begin to roll toward the hole. It came to a stop about six inches away from the hole.

That was the greatest shot I'd ever hit. Eugene hit one onto the green and putted twice. I tapped my putt into the cup for a birdie.

Now, I'd love to tell you that I had the best round ever that day and that I'd shattered the course record, but that's just not how golf works. I played okay for the rest of the day. I made a few more pars and sunk a twenty-five-foot putt on the fourteenth green. But for that one hole, for just a few shots, I was a great golfer. I'd never been great at anything in my life before. I was good in English class, very good at making people laugh, and an above-average video-game player. But never in my life had I felt as if I'd mastered something, even for a moment. Swinging that club and hitting that ball perfectly made me feel better than I'd ever felt before. I had never experienced a rush like the rush I got watching that ball roll toward the hole. And I wanted more.

I started to think that maybe this was just the beginning for me in golf. Maybe I could make a career out of this. After all, I'd only been playing for a few months and I was getting better each day. If I continued to work hard and improve, maybe I could play in high school, then college, and someday even pro tournaments. Sure, it was a tough road, but I'd never had a dream before, and now that I had one, my life started to make much more sense. I was moving toward something. I wasn't just a goofball anymore, I was somebody who wanted to be something special—a professional golfer.

So, you can understand why I was so excited when Harvey told me that professional golfers were going to be coming to Whispering Canyon. After all, if I wanted to be one, I needed to at least know what they looked like and how well they played. The Invitational Classic was coming to town in a few weeks. The Classic is a pretty big deal in the golf world. It's a tournament that travels around the country. What's so special about it is that local players get paired up with a professional player. Only the best local players get selected for the tournament, which explains the invitational part of the name. Eugene says it's a big honor to be selected for the Invitational Classic. It's like being a professional amateur.

The fact that the tournament was coming to Whispering Canyon was also a big deal. The Invitational Classic is held at the best public course in the area, so that means Whispering Canyon was one of the best golf courses in Washington. Everyone at the course was excited that we were selected to host the event, and everyone in town said that we owed it all to Harvey. Doug, the head lawn-care specialist, was quoted in the local newspaper saying, "No one has done more to make this course great than Harvey. He took a poorly run, poorly designed course and almost single-handedly turned it into one of the best public golf courses in the state. And that young fellow who's always with him, Eugene, he's done an awful lot for the course too." Eugene was very excited that his name was mentioned in the newspaper. He cut out the article and pinned it to the wall in his room.

In the weeks leading up to the event, there was a buzz around town. One night at dinner, Dad mentioned reading about the tournament, "I haven't been to the Invitational Classic since it came to town back in," he paused and scrunched his nose, "Gosh, how long ago was that?" Dad always scrunched in his nose when he was thinking. Kind of like Eugene staring up at the sky. I wondered if I had a thinking face.

Mom chimed in. She had the most amazing memory. "That was thirty years ago, next Saturday. It was cloudy and the wind kept blowing your hat off your head. Remember?"

Dad's memory was magically jogged, "Yup, I remember now. That was the first time I ever saw a professional golfer in real life."

"So what are they like?" I asked curiously.

"Actually, I remember being kind of let down."

"Really?" I asked.

"Well, they're little guys." Dad took a tiny bite of his chicken. "Now don't laugh, but I used to play football. Up until fourth grade. I was never any good—as you might imagine—but I was fast. Anyway, as a special treat, at the end of the season, we all got to go to a real college football game at the University of Washington stadium. All us little football kids were allowed onto the field to meet the players. I remember looking up at them, in all their pads and helmets, and thinking to myself, 'These aren't real people, they're giants.' But when my father took me to the Invitational Classic, and I got to see the pro golfers for the first time up close, I remember looking at them and thinking, 'These guys all look just like my dad.' And you know why I remember that, Jason?"

"No, not really," I spoke through a mouthful of mashed potatoes.

"Because that's another thing that's so great about golf. You can't tell how good someone is just by looking at them. If you see a nine-foot-tall man walking down the street, chances are that fellow's going to be good at basketball. But the best golfer in the world could walk right by you, and you'd have no idea." Dad was right. I'd never thought about that before. That's probably why golf was so appealing to me, a chubby kid with carpet hair. It was the only sport I'd ever played where guys like Calvin couldn't just beat me out because they were better athletes.

Dad took a large sip of water. "Can you get me some cheap tickets, Jason?"

"Probably, Dad," I said.

"Great."

Another exciting part of the Invitational Classic was the Youth Pairs Tournament. You pair up with someone your own age and compete against other people in the same age group. To win your age group in the Invitational Classic Youth Pairs Tournament is a pretty neat thing, because besides getting a big trophy, you automatically become one of the golfers who will be selected to play with a pro if the tour ever comes to town again. It's like winning something that could last for fifty years.

I was surprised to hear Calvin talking about the tournament at lunch. "I think I'm going to enter the Youth Pairs Tournament," he said.

"You're going to enter?" This thought excited me for a minute. Maybe Calvin and I could be partners. I was sure he'd be impressed by how much better I had gotten. Then I remembered that Calvin didn't even like golf. "I thought you hated golf," I said.

"I never said that. It's just not as cool as football. But it would be pretty cool to win a tournament. I like to win."

"Yeah, I know," I said. Calvin was like that. Anything athletic he tried, he was great at it. His mother was a really big golfer, so Calvin had been golfing since he was four years old. He didn't play very much, but he was still good. I stuffed a sugar snap pea into my mouth and prepared to ask Calvin to be my partner.

Just as this thought entered into my head, Calvin spoke, "Dave Codura and I are going to enter together."

I almost choked on the pea I was eating when he said that. "You and Dave are going to be partners?" I asked.

"Yeah," said Calvin. "We were talking about it in history class. Dave's a pretty good golfer. Because of the car dealership, Dave's dad is always going to or sponsoring some kind of golf tournament. Dave gets to play in a bunch of them. He's been doing it for a long time. We think we can win."

"Hmm," I said. "Well, good luck."

Calvin looked at me for a second. I think he could tell I was a little upset. "You didn't want to play in the tournament, did you Jason? I mean, you haven't been playing golf that long and you're not exactly the best athlete."

That comment really ticked me off. "Well, I've been playing a little bit at work and I'm kind of getting the hang of it."

"I didn't know you were playing. I thought you were just there cleaning golf balls. If I'd known that you were getting into golf, we could have been partners." *Yeah, right,* I thought. "But you know, Dave and I already agreed to form a pair, so I couldn't back out on him or anything," said Calvin.

"Mark Brotherton can partner up with you, he hits the ball a long way."

"No, that's cool," I said. There was no chance I was going to pair up with Mark Brotherton. I'd rather eat my own shoes. "I don't even think I'm going to enter the tournament. It's not really my thing. You know I'm not much for competition." Even as I was saying those words, which were partially true, my feelings were still hurt that Calvin didn't ask to be my partner. It was just like when he paired up with Dave in history class. Here I was, Calvin's supposed friend for eight years, but when a chance to do something with someone cooler than me came up, our friendship never seemed to count.

At work later that day Eugene and I were repairing the skirt around hole fourteen. The skirt is the area in between the fairway and the green. It's not quite the green, but it's not quite the fairway either. The skirt is hard to maintain. It's cut differently than the fairway—the grass is mowed much closer to the ground. The skirt gets damaged more easily than the fairway too, so Eugene and I were reseeding some bare parts and doing our best to fix the small holes that are inevitably made from clubs and golf shoes. Before I worked at Whispering Canyon, I had no idea how much effort went into maintaining a golf course. I still couldn't get over how much work it took to run. It's a lot more than just watering a bunch of grass.

Like everyone else at the course these days, Eugene and I were talking about the Invitational Classic. Eugene was getting very excited. He knew all the players in the tournament, he memorized the schedule of events, and he even knew which local players were paired up with which professionals.

He was a walking encyclopedia of golf tournament information.

"Did you know that Sidney Fathers is going to be playing here?" he asked.

"No, I didn't," I said. It's true, I really didn't know that Sidney Fathers was going to be playing at the tournament. I also didn't know who the heck Sidney Fathers was, but Eugene didn't need to know that.

"Pretty exciting, huh?"

"Yeah, really exciting." Sometimes you just had to humor Eugene. "So, do you think that you're going to play in the youth tournament?" I had been thinking about asking Eugene to be my partner since Calvin told me he was going to play with Dave Codura. The truth was, I should have asked Eugene in the first place! Lately, he'd been more of a best friend than Calvin ever had been to me. Plus (and nobody at school knew this), he was by far the best junior golfer around.

Eugene looked at me and then quickly looked away. All of the sudden he was looking more awkward than usual, which is saying a lot for Eugene.

"What's the matter?" I asked.

"Well, you see," Eugene stammered, "I, uh, I don't like to play in front of a lot of people. It makes me too nervous. I mean really, really nervous. Once, Harvey got me to play in this little tournament down in Tacoma and I threw up all over the first tee. It was pretty disgusting. So I don't think I'm going to be playing in a tournament anytime soon. But you should play. You've been doing really well for how long you've been playing. I bet that we could find a partner that you could team up with. It would be fun."

"Nah, that's okay. I think I'll just watch this time around too." I paused. "I've never been one for tournaments or the spotlight either." There was a long, awkward silence as we continued to reseed the grass. I knew that I needed to make a great speech. Something that would get Eugene so fired up that he wouldn't be able to not play in the tournament. Something that would inspire him to be my partner and win the whole thing. Instead I said, "You're a weirdo, Eugene. Everyone at school thinks so. And I'm a complete joke. They laugh *at* me, not with me." Eugene stopped reseeding and stared at me. "Wouldn't it be something if the weird kid and the fat kid beat out the cool kids and took home the trophy? Wouldn't that just be perfect?"

There was a long silence. I hoped that I hadn't hurt Eugene's feelings. Finally, he smiled, "I *am* a weirdo."

I laughed, grabbing a pile of flab from my stomach, "And I'm still pretty chunky, Eugene." I paused, "So will you be my partner and we can beat out Calvin and those other guys?"

"Sure, but I might puke, Jason."

"And I might eat three sandwiches by the ninth hole."

We both laughed hysterically, reseeding the skirt in preparation for the tournament.

CHAPTER TEN

THE MINI GOLF DISASTER

The clown was mocking me.

He was taunting me with his big stupid smile. "Jason, your putting is a joke. Your game is funny, but sad funny, not funny-funny like me," said the clown. Well, he didn't actually say that out loud, but I could tell he was thinking it. And I hated him for that. I imagined smashing his big stupid red nose in with my putter.

The clown's head was the fourth hole at Wild Bob's Funderful Fun Park. Eugene was already beating me very badly—I had shot nine strokes compared to his five—and it didn't look like things would get better any time soon. Eugene had just made a beautiful putt that went through the clown's mouth, down to the second level, and landed about two inches from the cup. He would score an easy two, no problem.

I was debating whether or not to try and go through the

clown's mouth like Eugene or to hug the side railing. The mouth shot was risky because the clown's jaw opened and closed every few seconds. This meant that not only did you have to line up the shot perfectly on his tongue, you also had to time your shot so that the ball wouldn't hit the clown's big ugly buckteeth and land right back at your feet. Going around the clown's head was a much easier shot. There was no chance that the ball would come back at you, but there was also no chance you'd get down to the second level in one shot. Blocks on either side of the path that led to the lower level prevented that. Your only shot at a hole in one was going through the clown's mouth.

No guts, no glory, I thought to myself, and smacked my putt. To my amazement, the ball rolled right up the clown's tongue. And as luck would have it, I timed the shot right. The golf ball disappeared down the clown's throat and made a few clanging sounds before ending up on the second level where it rolled toward the cup. The only thing between my orange ball and a hole in one was Eugene's yellow ball.

No, it couldn't happen. It wouldn't happen. It shouldn't happen. But then it happened. My golf ball tapped Eugene's ball right into the hole.

"Huh," said Eugene. "I guess that's a hole in one for me." He walked down to the lower level to pick up his golf ball. Eugene was amazing. He was an incredible golfer but the least competitive person I ever met. He wasn't even keeping score. He was killing me, and he wasn't even keeping score. Things kept going on like this until my whole universe came crashing in at hole seven.

There's nothing particularly special about hole seven.

It's the medieval hole. They call it the medieval hole because there's a big castle in the middle of it. The castle's drawbridge opens and closes just like the clown's mouth on hole four. If you miss the drawbridge or don't time your shot right, your ball will land in the moat and wind up behind a cement dragon, instead of right in front of the hole. It's a tough shot getting around the dragon, so you really want to make the drawbridge.

Of course, Eugene made the shot right away. I got lucky, and also made the shot. "Nice shot," said Eugene. We walked down past the dragon to see where our golf balls landed. When we rounded the corner, I saw a very disturbing sight. Calvin and Mark Brotherton were paired up with Sandie and Debbie Harris, and they were only two holes ahead of us.

Sandie and Debbie were identical twins and the best-looking girls in school, or I guess I should say the best-looking girl in school, since they looked exactly the same. I always got them mixed up. Personally, I didn't think either of them was very nice, but they were extremely popular (mostly because of their long blonde hair). They had a lot of influence over who was included in the popular crowd, so I usually tried to stay on their good side—steering clear of them as much as possible.

Either Sandie or Debbie had a crush on Calvin. The other one liked Mark, which is no surprise. Girls loved Mark. Which poses the question: why do girls always like the biggest jerks? That's a mystery I don't think I'll ever be able to solve.

Calvin was the first one in the group to spot me. I saw him do a double take to make sure it was me. He looked a little confused, as I don't think he'd ever seen me with Eugene.

"Hey, Jason," he called out.

"Oh, what's up, Calvin?" I said, acting excited to see him as I made my way over. Eugene stayed back at the medieval hole.

"Hi, Jason," said Sandie or Debbie.

"Hi," I said.

"So, what is this, Take-a-Dork-to-Mini-Golf Day?" Mark asked. He started laughing and the rest of the group joined him. Man, Mark was a jerk. I didn't know how to answer, so I didn't say anything. Mark kept going, "I think I saw a sign out front that said if you bring a nerd to play mini-golf, you get half price on admission." Mark was laughing again, along with the rest of them. I could see Eugene out of the corner of my eye. He was standing next to my ball, waiting for me to come back and putt. I was sure he was hearing all of this. I didn't know what to do. I just wanted to get away from the whole situation. "Hey Eugene!" Mark shouted. "I like your glasses!"

"C'mon, Mark," I said. "Cut it out." That was all I could think of to say. I don't think that in the history of people trying to get out of bad situations, the words "cut it out" have ever worked. But that's all I could think of to say. I'm sure Mark has heard those words many times in a lifelong mission filled with bullying and belittling. So I wasn't surprised when he didn't skip a beat.

"Cut what out?" He asked me. "All I'm trying to figure out is why you'd rather spend time with," and he yelled this part so Eugene could hear him, "THE BIGGEST LOSER IN THE SCHOOL when you could be hanging out with us."

"Eugene's cooler than you'll ever be, Mark. When you're forty years old and fat and bald and coming home after

94

a long day of digging holes for minimum wage, you'll sit down on your filthy couch and turn on your broken TV and you'll see Eugene's face. The reporter will say, 'World-renowned scientist Eugene Jewel cures world hunger with the perfection of his photosynthetic, lactose-free cheese. We go live to Joyce Garner for the Nobel Peace Prize press conference.' And you'll remember how you used to make fun of Eugene and how cool you were and what a dork he was, and you'll see what a life-time of being a first-class jerk got you, and what a lifetime of being a genius got Eugene. And it will hurt. It will hurt bad." That's what I wanted to say. That's what I wished I'd said.

But this is what I actually said, "C'mon Mark. I just work with him is all." The words fell out of my mouth the way a dinner glass falls off the edge of a table.

"So come on and play with us then," said Calvin.

"Yeah, play along with us, Jason," said Debbie or Sandie, flicking her blonde hair over her shoulder.

I looked back at Eugene and we made eye contact with one another. The moment of truth had arrived. And I can't be-lieve I did this, but I left Eugene at the medieval hole to go golf with the cool kids. I left him standing there alone next to the castle, completely humiliated. I didn't even go to pick up my orange ball.

I couldn't sleep that night. I just lay in my bed and stared at the ceiling. I thought about calling up Eugene and apologiz-ing, but it was too late. I kept playing the mini-golf scene over and over again in my head. I kept leaving Eugene, over and over. I kept choosing the kids that everyone thought were cool instead of the kid that was really my friend. Eugene had never been anything but nice to me, but the first chance I got, I went and rubbed his face in what a nerd he was and how much better I thought I was than him.

This had been the happiest six months of my entire life. I'd found my first true friend and I fell in love with the game of golf and got pretty good at it too. I was starting to actually feel good about myself and was losing weight. So why would I do something like that to Eugene, the guy who helped me realize who I really was? Why was I such a coward that I couldn't stand up to those jerks? Was fitting in that important to me? Important enough to hurt my friend? Important enough to keep me from what I really wanted to do? And the only answer I could come up with was yes. It really was that important to me. Suddenly, I felt bad about myself all over again. I jumped out of bed and ran downstairs to eat a bowl of ice cream.

I didn't see Eugene at school the next day. He wasn't eating lunch in his normal spot, and I didn't pass him in the halls. I didn't see him at school the day after that either, and by this time, I was really looking for him. I didn't know what I would say when I found him, but it seemed important to talk to him. I figured I would have to run into him at work that afternoon anyway.

When I got to the golf course I checked in with Phil, as usual. "Hey Phil," I said.

Phil looked up from the table. He was wearing one of those jeweler's glasses over his left eye. His eye was a gigantic bloodshot ball. He was holding a square of sandpaper in his left hand and a Q-tip in the other. As usual, I didn't have to ask

Phil what he was doing.

"I've been here all night, sanding down every fifth dimple. I'm on to something here, Jason. As you know, I've been thinking a lot about fractals. According to my calculations, sanding down every fifth dimple will improve the aerodynamics of the ball by twenty-six percent. That means longer drives, Jason. I can't believe I haven't thought about it until now. It's so simple. It's just so simple." Next to the golf ball Phil was sanding sat a notebook with all kinds of complicated-looking calculations. Phil noticed me looking at his notebook and quickly shut it and placed it into a box that he locked right in front of me.

"Fractals, that's great, Phil," I said. "So, have you seen Eugene?"

"Eugene's sick today," he said. "But I did see Harvey. He told me he wants you to meet him at hole three."

"Thanks," I said, and I left Phil to his sanding.

Harvey was on the green of hole three. He was moving the flag from the front of the hole to the back.

"Hi Harvey," I said.

"Hello, Jason," said Harvey. He didn't look up at me. "Could you please hand me my leveler from the toolbox?" I went over to his toolbox and pulled out his leveler. Whenever Harvey made a new hole, he always took out his leveler and measured the slope of the green. He didn't care if the hole was level or not, but he always measured it, just so he'd know.

"Here you go," I said, handing him the leveler.

"Thank you," said Harvey. He looked up at me and sighed deeply, "Well, today is your last day at Whispering

Canyon, Jason."

He'd spoken those words so casually that I nearly missed them entirely. "Excuse me?" I asked.

"Today is your last day here," said Harvey. He wasn't looking at me now, his concentration was back on hole three.

"But, uh, why?" I asked.

Harvey put his notebook in his back pocket and put the leveler down on the ground. "It's clear that you don't want to be here. And I don't want your negative energy on my course."

"What negative energy? I love it here."

"For six months, I've taught you, Jason. I've taught you about the greatest game in the world, which is golf. And you have learned well. Probably faster than anyone I've taught before. But what I didn't notice until now, was that while you were getting down the mechanics, you completely missed the spirit of the game. Golf is more than just a sport. It changes the way you look at the world and how you look at yourself.

"After what happened with Eugene, it's clear that you're not growing inside. Perhaps it's my fault. Perhaps I was expecting too much. Whatever the reason, I don't want you here anymore. I thought you were different than the kid who pulled a stupid prank at the fair, but I guess I was mistaken.

"And by the way, you should know that Eugene tried not to say anything to me. I saw how upset he was and pulled it out of him. I thought you understood what a sensitive young man he is. You know that he doesn't have a lot of friends and that he's very careful with whom he gets close to. He let you into his world and you broke his trust.

"I'll honor the obligation I made to your parents about

providing you with work. I've spoken with a friend who owns Dan's Sandwiches downtown. Dan said that he can use the help and you can keep your same hours. I'm sure you'll figure out something to say to your parents to explain why you have a new job." With that, Harvey put his leveler back in his toolbox and stood up, looking at me. "You can have the rest of the day off. Goodbye, Jason."

When he finished talking, I didn't know what to say. So I left. I took a long time getting home that afternoon. I rode my bike all over the neighborhood. I didn't know where I was headed, I just kept riding. I rode past the school, past downtown, past Dan's Sandwiches, past the post office, over the North Bend Bridge, and up Gallagher Hill. It felt good to be riding. I didn't think of anything, I was just moving. I didn't realize how long I had been riding until I wound up at the Henderson Farm. The Henderson Farm is a pretty good drive from my house, so it kind of spooked me when I realized how far I'd gone. I looked at my watch. I'd been riding for over two hours. I was supposed to be home in another two, so I turned my bike around and started to head back.

I passed this little field on my way back. The field was full of clover. An old horse toward the back of the field was eating the clover. For some reason, I thought it might make me feel better to go talk to the horse. I leaned my bike against the fence that enclosed the field, and very carefully made my way through the barbed wire.

I don't have much experience with horses. I was always amazed by them, though, especially by how fast they peed. It was like hyperpee. I always appreciated that about horses. I approached the horse from the front, remembering that you're not supposed to ever approach a horse from behind because you could scare it and it could kick you, and it would probably be the last time you ever sneaked up on a horse. So I went around the front of the horse. He was old and gray. He stood hunched over, quietly chewing on the clover.

"Hey, old horse," I said. The horse didn't look up at me. It just kept chewing the clover. "I got fired today. Just like that, I got fired. I used to work on a golf course. I was learning how to play golf. I was actually getting good at it too. Do you know what it's like to be decent at something? Looks like you might have been a pretty fast runner back in your day. I bet it felt pretty great to run fast, huh?" Still, no response from the horse, but I kept on talking. "I've never really been good at anything until I started that job. I'd never had a real friend either. But then I went and did something stupid and messed it all up." I paused for effect, "And I'm not even upset that I got fired. I deserved it. I'm just upset that I knew what I was supposed to do in the situation, and I did the exact opposite. I should have stayed with Eugene. I should have told that jerk Mark to get lost and leave us alone. I know that now. The bad thing is, I knew it then, too."

I thought I saw the horse nod his head like he was trying to tell me something, but it turned out that he was just crushing an extra-big bite of clover. I patted him on the head and started to smile. Then, just when I thought my day couldn't get any worse, I heard a strange noise, like someone had just turned on the shower in Mom and Dad's bathroom. When I looked down, I realized that the horse had started to pee, soaking my right leg and both of my shoes.

It was a long, cold, bike ride home.

CHAPTER ELEVEN

LET'S DO IT

I already knew that I couldn't control time, so there was no stopping the next Wednesday from rolling around. When the day came, instead of going to Whispering Canyon, I took a different bus to Dan's Sandwiches. Since I'd be working the same hours that I did at the golf course, I didn't feel the need to tell my parents that I had a new job. Even though I knew that lying to them always got me into trouble, I just couldn't bring myself to tell them how I'd ruined my friendship with Eugene and given up on golf.

Things at Dan's Sandwiches were okay, I guess. Dan was a nice guy. He looked to be about the same age as Harvey but he was much bigger. He had thick, hairy arms that popped out of the dirty white T-shirt he wore under his dirty white apron. Dan had curly black hair that he kept covered in a paper hat. Despite his hair-control efforts, every once in a while, I would serve up a tuna sandwich with extra curly black hair.

When I came to work, the first thing Dan gave me was an apron. The apron was definitely used. Stains from who knows when had taken up permanent residence in the thick cotton. "Here's your apron. Please keep it on at all times when you're working." Hairy Dan was serious about sanitation. Then Dan gave me a paper hat like the one he wore. "Here's your hat. Please keep it on at all times when you're working. And always wash your hands. A clean deli is a healthy deli."

I mostly cleaned the counters, handed out sandwiches, and sliced pickles. Like I said, it was okay. After working with Phil, I could probably handle any job. But still, standing next to hairy Dan while slices of salami shot by my ears like hand grenades really made me want to go back to working at the golf course. I wanted to be out there among the trees with Eugene and Harvey, working on the greens, planning where to put the holes, and playing golf. I wanted to keep learning from Harvey and I wanted to hang out with Eugene. I wanted us to be friends again.

I hadn't seen Eugene for about a week. I looked everywhere for him, but he was doing an amazing job of avoiding me. Finally, I caught him walking out of his English class. He was at the other side of the hall, carrying a large stack of books. He glanced across at me, then quickly turned his head away as if we hadn't made eye contact at all. He began walking much faster, staring down at the ground as he passed me.

"Hey, Eugene," I said, trying to keep up with him.

He looked up at me, and the look in his face was one that I will never forget. He didn't look mad at me; there was no hate in his eyes. He just looked kind of hollow, like nothing was there.

"Hey, man," I said, again, trying to get him to acknowledge that he knew who I was. "I know you probably don't want to talk to me right now, and I understand. But I just wanted to say I'm sorry. That was a really terrible thing for me to do. I've thought a lot about it and I know that I was wrong, and I'll never do anything to you like that again." The words I spoke were the truth, but I understood when Eugene didn't seem to believe them. I hadn't given him any reason to believe them.

Eugene continued to look at me blankly. It made me uncomfortable, so I kept talking. "The tournament's coming up. We're still partners, right? The fat kid and the weirdo winning the whole thing, right?" Eugene wouldn't say a word. I lowered my voice, "Forget the tournament. I'd just like to be friends again. I'm so sorry. I know it was a really, really, really bad thing to do." I was waiting for him to say something, anything, but he wouldn't. "If it makes you feel any better, I got fired from Whispering Canyon, so you won't have to bump into me there any more."

Eugene stared at me for a second. His eyes were welling up with tears. "I saw you."

"Excuse me," I said.

"I saw you, Jason."

"You saw me when?"

"I saw you watching when Mark broke my glasses outside of the girls' bathroom. I saw you standing there and doing nothing."

"You saw me?" I hung my head in shame.

"Yeah. I never said anything because we weren't really friends yet. But then you did it again to me, Jason. And this time, we were friends, at least that's what I thought."

"We are friends."

"Maybe we were, but not anymore. That jerk Mark smashed my glasses. He makes my life awful. He pushes me in the hall. He and Tommy think it's the funniest thing in the world to prank phone call my house and scare my mother. Do you know what it's like having to explain to your parents why sixteen pizzas were delivered to your house? Do you know what it's like having to lie to your dad about accidentally smashing your glasses because you're too ashamed to tell him they were destroyed by Mark? Do you know how hard it is for me here, Jason? I hate this place. And then I think that I've finally made a friend, someone who I really like—I should have known you would ditch me the first chance you got. But to ditch me and go hang out with Mark, that was just too much." Eugene stopped for a moment. "With Mark," he repeated.

"Look, Eugene. I made a big mistake. I feel horrible. Isn't there anything I can do to make it up to you?"

I could tell Eugene was trying not to cry. "Yeah, you can find a new partner for the tournament and never speak to me again." With that he walked down the hall, escaping down the crowded hallway.

I felt lower than dirt. Like the layer of earth underneath the dirt, I think it's called the magma or something. Yup, I felt like a pile of magma.

With Eugene out of the picture, things over the next

month or so returned back to normal. Or I guess I should say the old normal. I spent most of my time with Calvin and the cool kids again. Not just during school, but on the weekends when I wasn't working too. Instead of lifting weights and practicing golf, I was hanging out at the mall and having eating competitions with big Leroy Willis outside of Rubino's Pizza. I ate nine slices in five minutes and threw up in the bathroom. That was bad. What was worse was that Leroy ate ten and beat me. I wasn't even good at being the fat kid anymore.

Gaining back some of the weight I lost was no fun. It was like watching myself go downhill and not being able to stop it. I didn't feel like working out anymore, and golf was just too expensive for me to play. Plus, it reminded me of Eugene and what I'd done to my only true friend.

Life at Dan's Sandwiches was fine. Besides cleaning the counters and slicing pickles, Dan had me shredding lettuce, baking bread, and even helping slice some of the meats and cheeses. It wasn't a bad job, but I still wished I was back at Whispering Canyon. Making a good sandwich didn't feel quite the same way as hitting a good golf shot.

The longer I worked at Dan's and hung out with the Calvin and the cool kids, the farther away Whispering Canyon got. After a month, it seemed like the whole golf thing was a distant chapter in my life that was over as suddenly as it had began. Every once in a while, I'd see Eugene in the halls. He'd avoid looking at me when I passed him, and it got to be like we were never friends in the first place.

I would spend my lunches at the popular table making Mark, Calvin, Debbie and/or Sandie, and anyone else who was eating laugh their heads off. I made fun of myself and usually left lunch feeling terrible. Like I said, things got back to normal. But no matter how normal everything was again, I couldn't help feeling that something was missing. And I wanted more than anything to right the wrong I caused Eugene. The only problem was, I had no idea how.

I decided I would go and watch the tournament anyway. Harvey may have fired me, but he never said that I was banned from the course. I wanted to see how Calvin and Dave would do. I wasn't going to cheer them on or even support them. I was just curious to see if they were going to be as good as they thought they would. I kind of wanted them to lose, but I was sure that with Eugene and I out of the tournament, they were probably the front-runners.

Although I wouldn't admit it, the bigger part of why I was going to the match was because I was hoping to see Eugene. We hadn't spoken in nearly a month, yet I still desperately wanted to find a way to make things right with us again. I knew he'd be there too. There was no chance that Eugene would miss the match, he loved golf too much. I thought that maybe being together again on the golf course would make it easier for Eugene to forgive me, but I wasn't holding my breath.

I walked into the main entrance of Whispering Canyon. It felt really weird being there as a spectator. I felt like I should go help Harvey with something. I even would have settled for cleaning some golf balls with Phil. But all I could do was watch what was going on as an outsider.

At the course, things were busier than I'd ever seen

them. It was the second day of the Invitational Classic, and the youth tournament was to be held today, the only daylong break from the adult tournament. I was surprised by how many people were there despite the big tournament not resuming play until the next day. The parents of the players were in the crowd. I also recognized a bunch of kids from school. Sally McCoy was there, and unfortunately I noticed Mark and Tommy in the crowd as well. There were also lots of other kids I didn't recognize, and most of the players from the Invitational Classic were there too. Since they had the day off, they probably didn't have anything better to do then watch a bunch of kids play golf. It turned out to be a much bigger event than I imagined. And of course, Phil was there to make it even bigger.

Phil was standing in the backdrop of the crowd, speaking into an old video camera, as if he were telecasting this event for ESPN. (He probably really thought he was.) "Hello, golf fans, and welcome to the Youth Pairs Tournament, the youth tournament of the Invitational Classic held here at Whispering Canyon Country Club. Judging by the incredible talent pool, it could shape up to be a very exciting day. We turn our camera to hole number one, as our first golfing twosome, Dave Codura and Calvin Anderson of the Codura/Anderson Team, prepare to tee off and start the day."

Patrick, a skinny high school kid with bad skin, wearing a pair of stained yellow cutoff sweatpants and a T-shirt that read "ALIENS ARE REAL," was holding the old video camera and pointing it at Phil. Judging by his appearance, I assumed this guy was somehow related to Phil. I later found out that I was right, the two were first cousins. Patrick turned his video camera on Dave at the first tee—and I mean right on him. Dave looked pretty uncomfortable.

Phil was standing behind the cameraman. He was wearing a light gray suit that was much too small for him. The pant legs only came down to his calves, revealing mismatched argyle socks. The sleeves on the jacket stopped at his forearms. The jacket was so tight, it made Phil scrunch up his body. Also, I should add, Phil was wearing a green-and-black-spotted bow tie. He looked ridiculous, but he was doing his best to take his job of golf commentator seriously.

A camera lens was about three inches from Dave's neck when Dave asked Patrick, "Can you back up, please?"

"Patrick!" snapped Phil. "Give the golfers some room there, will ya?"

Patrick backed up a few feet and Dave took his shot. Phil commentated, "Well, golf fans, it looks like things are off to a great start with a beautiful shot from young Codura. Let's see if Dave's partner, Calvin Anderson, can better him."

There's one thing that needs some explaining here. Phil asked if Calvin could beat Dave because the Youth Pairs Tournament is what is known in the golf world as a scramble. The way a scramble works is that you play from the best shot of whomever is on your team. So if Calvin hit a shot that landed closer to the hole than Dave, both players would play their next shot from where Calvin's golf ball landed. If Calvin hit a bad shot, they would both play from Dave's shot. Playing in a scramble is pretty fun because there's a backup if you really mess up a shot. But if both you and your partner really mess up, then you're in trouble.

Calvin stepped up to the tee with Patrick's lens a few inches away from his face. "Hey, back up you freak!" Calvin snapped angrily. The more I saw Calvin interact with the rest of the world, the more I realized that calling him my best friend was not something I should be proud of.

Patrick answered, "I just want the people watching at home to really feel the emotion here." This was a strange comment for a number of reasons. First of all, there were no viewers at home. Patrick was taping with Phil's video camera and the only people who would ever watch the video were going to be Phil and Patrick. Also, how can sticking a camera six inches from someone's face make you feel their emotion? The only thing Patrick was going to feel was the back of Calvin's driver hitting him in the head when he swung.

So Patrick backed up a few feet and Calvin teed up. He took three practice swings then approached the ball. Calvin's real swing was much faster than his practice swing. I've noticed that a lot in golf. People will make lots of perfect practice swings, but when it comes time for the real swing, they get nervous and move too fast. When you swing too fast, you lose control of the club. Calvin's shot veered way off to the right. He got a lot of distance on it, but the ball landed in the deep rough. Calvin muttered something under his breath that I couldn't hear. I know it was wrong of me, but I felt a little happy when Calvin hit a bad shot. He never did anything poorly.

"Oh, and the Codura/Anderson team is dealt a devastating blow," commented Phil. "It's a good thing Codura set the pair up so nicely, or they would be in real trouble. We now turn our attention to the Hosik/Beakman team. Let's see how things unfold."

Two kids I didn't know came out from the crowd. As they emerged, I noticed Eugene hiding near the back of the audience. He was by himself, watching the match from a distance. Across the crowd from Eugene, I noticed Mark and Tommy making their way toward him. Quickly, Tommy ran behind Eugene while Mark walked up to him. Why wouldn't they just leave him alone?

In a moment of bravery, without thinking, I raced over to them. Tommy was kneeling on the ground behind Eugene, and from the looks of it, Mark was going to push Eugene over and completely embarrass him. This was pretty standard double-team bully procedure. When someone pushes you and you don't know that someone else is kneeling down behind you, you fall all the way to the ground, and you usually fall pretty hard. To be honest, it seemed pretty mild for Mark and Tommy, but still, enough was enough.

"Hey, Eugene," said Mark, walking up to him. "Why aren't you playing? I thought golf was your favorite sport. It always made sense to me that the lamest person in the school would like the lamest sport in the world."

Eugene started to back up away from Mark and he was just about to trip over Tommy. Until I came out of nowhere.

"There you are," I shouted to Eugene.

Mark, Tommy, and Eugene looked at me with total confusion.

"Come on, we're going to be late," I said to Eugene. "We're about to start." I looked over at Mark, "Eugene and I are partners today. We're almost up." I looked down at Tommy on the ground. "What are you doing on the ground Tommy?" I talked to him like he was a little kid. I knew he had a complex about being so small, so I knew this would really get under his skin. "Did Big Mark make you get on the ground or did you lose something? Maybe Mark dropped his little brain, that'll sure be tough to find. Actually, maybe you guys should check the pro shop and see if they have a magnifying glass." Tommy angrily looked up at me and Mark was steaming. "Seriously though, if you two morons will excuse us, we have a tournament to win." I looked over at Eugene, "Eugene, are you ready to play?"

With Mark and Tommy ready to kill me, the moment of truth had arrived. Either way, at this point, I had written myself a one-way ticket out of the popular crowd, and possibly a one-way ticket to a black eye. I knew it. Mark knew it. Tommy knew it. And I think Eugene did too. I stared over at Eugene and smiled, feeling like a weight had been lifted off my back. I'd finally stood up to the cool kids, and being true to myself felt great.

Eugene looked down at Tommy and then back to me. He smiled back at me, "Oh yeah, I totally forgot. Let's go, Jason." The two of us walked away quickly from Mark and Tommy, who had now placed me on the top of their list of people they were going to torment. I'd saved Eugene. I only hoped this would make up for the mini-golf disaster.

"Thanks," said Eugene. "That was great."

"No problem," I said. "Felt pretty good to tell those guys off. I should have done it a long time ago." I paused, watching someone else tee off. "So, you wanna really do it?"

"Do what?" asked Eugene.

"Play in the youth tournament. I mean, I haven't played in a month, but—"

"I don't know," said Eugene, cutting me off. Even though I had helped him get away from Mark and Tommy, he was still kind of mad at me, and he was terrified of golfing in front of other people.

"Look, I'm really sorry about the way I've treated you. I feel awful about it every day. If I could go back in time and change everything, I would. But I can't. But think about it, Eugene, we could be playing golf together again. No matter how mad at me you are, you're still missing out on a chance to play your favorite game. And you're missing out on a chance to win. I promise I won't leave you this time. I promise I'll be a better friend from now on."

Eugene scrunched up his eyebrows and looked at me. Then he looked at the golf course. Then he looked over at Mark and Tommy. Mark was giving Tommy a giant wedgie and hanging him on a tree branch. "Let's do it."

CHAPTER TWELVE

KICKING BUTT

"We'd like to make a last minute addition," I said.

"The tournament is closed. The deadline to enter was last Friday."

The woman working the information table looked like the kind of person who didn't think many things in life were funny. Her hair was pulled back so tightly that it made her eyebrows rise high on her forehead. It gave her a look of constant angry surprise.

"Can't you make an exception for us?"

"No, I cannot make an exception," said Mrs. Tighthairsurprise. "You boys are out of luck. The tournament is closed. You gentlemen should have thought of entering back when everyone else did."

I was trying to figure out a way to sweet-talk the lady into letting us play, when out of nowhere, Eugene starts talking like I've never heard him talk before.

"Listen, Mrs.," Eugene looked at her name badge, "Beltzendohoover." That was a tongue twister. "Do you know who I am?"

"No, I do not," snapped Mrs. Beltzendohoover.

"Then, I guess you don't know who my father is either."

"No." Mrs. Beltzendohoover said.

"Does the name Sir Walter Stanley Jewel mean anything to you?" asked Eugene.

"I'm very busy here," said Mrs. Beltzendohoover. "I don't have time for any more of this silly little game. Now, I suggest you boys leave me alone, or I will have you removed from the course."

"Okay, Eugene. You heard the lady, let's go." What was Eugene doing? I couldn't get in trouble again, especially with my parents in the gallery.

Eugene turned to me and gave me a quick wink and said to her, "Sir Walter Stanley Jewel is not only the designer of the course we are standing on, but he is the world-renowned designer of over thirty award-winning golf courses. We just flew in from a delightful course in Scotland. Father never would miss the Invitational Classic. He's very excited to watch me play. It would be a shame for him to find out that his son wasn't allowed to play in the Youth Pairs Tournament because a certain woman wouldn't allow him to enter the tournament at the last minute. And it would also be a shame for my father not to make his annual contribution to Whispering Canyon because of the way his son was treated. Wouldn't that be a shame?"

asked Eugene. "Especially when all that woman had to do was let two thirteen-year-olds enter a silly little golf match."

Mrs. Betlzendohoover was completely buying Eugene's story. It was amazing. "I am sorry, Mr. Jewel. I had no idea that you just came in from Scotland." She fumbled for some papers. "Here, you two just have to fill out these forms and you can head out to hole one. Most of the players haven't teed off yet. You should have no problems entering."

We filled out the forms and Mrs. Beltzendohoover gave us a pass to get on the course. We walked away from the information tent and headed to hole one.

"That was amazing, Eugene," I said. "How did you do that?"

"Well," Eugene said, "I just figured it was time."

"Time for what," I asked.

"Sometimes, Jason, it's just time to kick a little butt. I don't know about you, but suddenly I feel like kicking butt." Who was this guy?

I didn't know where all this was coming from. I had never seen this side of Eugene before. "Me too," I said. "I'd love to kick some butt."

"So let's go win this thing," said Eugene as we walked to hole one.

Lots of people were surprised to see Eugene and me at the first hole. Calvin and Dave were surprised. Harvey was surprised. But I don't think anyone was as surprised as Phil.

"What's this? Folks, it looks like we have some very exciting news! Local favorite Eugene Jewel and wildcard Jason Green have entered the tournament at the eleventh hour.

This is a very unexpected twist to an already complex tournament. I know I'm speaking for every individual here when I say that things just got a little more interesting. What will happen? Who will win? Only time will tell. We now turn our attention to Jason Green as he tees off for the Jewel/Green team."

I stepped up to the tee box. I hadn't swung a golf club in a while so I was pretty stiff when I took my practice swings. My head was a little congested with thoughts like, Do I remember how to do this? Luckily, once I approached the ball, everything came back to me. Even though I wasn't wearing my golf shoes, and even though I was playing with borrowed clubs, everything felt right. I looked down the fairway at my target, tried to empty my head, took aim, and swung.

Things might have felt right, but they certainly didn't go right with the first swing. The ball took off and flew almost at a ninety-degree angle from the tee. It flew over the crowd and landed in the fountain behind the clubhouse. I turned bright red with embarrassment.

Mark Brotherton shouted at me from the gallery, "Nice shot, fatso." I tried to ignore him, but the truth was, his comment had shaken me up.

"Just ignore him," Eugene said, as he walked past me on the way to the tee box.

"Oh my," said Phil. "It is now up to Eugene on this first shot."

Eugene stepped up to the tee, and I could see Dave and Calvin looking back at us from two holes ahead. Eugene set his ball down and closed his eyes for a moment. He didn't look as nervous as I thought he would. He held his lunch down this time too, which was great news, especially for Patrick whose camera was about two feet away from Eugene. There was something different in Eugene's eyes. I think something changed in him when he decided to kick a little butt. Mrs. Beltzendohoover had set a fire in Eugene's belly and there was no way anyone was going to put it out. He opened his eyes and looked down the course. He brought his focused gaze back to the ball and took his swing.

It was beautiful, both the swing and the shot. The ball flew in a perfect arc right over the fairway. It flew over every other golf ball, bounced twice, rolled for a while, then stopped in a perfect position. Calvin and Dave looked worried. I felt a sense of calm cover me like a blanket.The game was underway.

Our next shot was about 150 yards to an elevated green. Eugene went first. He struck his seven iron perfectly. The ball was heading right for the flag, but a slight breeze moved it from left to right and it landed on the edge of the green. Then we got some bad luck. The ball started rolling with the slope of the green and ended up burying itself in a sand trap. It was up to me.

Now, my first shot had given me no confidence whatsoever, so I needed to clear my head for the second shot. Harvey used to say that the hardest shot in golf was the shot you hit after you missed one. Knowing this, I focused on forgetting my last shot. I looked over at Harvey in the gallery. Just before I hit, I thought about his question. I even heard his voice in my head, What do you see in front of you, Jason? And suddenly, I was a golfer again. I didn't see the trees or the mountains anymore, and I didn't notice Mark Brotherton giving me the finger from the gallery. Instead, I saw a spot on the green right near the flag.

I took my practice swings and approached the ball. I set my grip, bent my knees, and let it rip. I heard the pinging sound that I'd heard that day when I watched The Twins tee off next to the Pair of Pain. I knew right when I hit it that we'd be putting on our next shot. And I was right. The ball landed softly on the green.

We had about a twenty-foot putt that broke from left to right. Eugene putted first and nailed it, starting our day off with a birdie. The crowd applauded wildly. I looked over and saw Mom and Dad hugging one another and waving to me. I stared over at Mark Brotherton, who was kicking dirt at a squirrel, and then I high-fived Eugene. We were on our way.

We were winning and I was playing well. But the truth was, it didn't matter how I was playing. By the sixth hole I realized that Eugene was even better than I thought. I could have been a blindfolded chimpanzee, and we would still be winning. Eugene was that good. He was like a machine. He was unstoppable. Nearly every shot he hit was perfect. He had a look of determination that I'd never seen before. I did my best just to keep up with him. It was great. We were crushing every other team. By the time we made it to the tenth hole, no one was even close to our score.

"Well golf fans, what an exciting nine holes it has been. It's only natural at the turn in the game to reflect on what has been and to look forward and ponder what may be in the future. From the very first hole, last-minute entries Eugene Jewel and Jason Green have taken a commanding lead. They are not only the best twosome on the course, but they look to be the best two players in the Juniors Classic. And what a joy to watch. Eugene appears to have entered what we in the golfing business call the golfer's mind. And Jason, who has only been playing golf for about six months, is really crushing the ball. These two have bright futures in golf ahead of them." I hoped that Phil was right. "Every other team at the moment is dwarfed by the prowess of the Jewel/Green team. The Codura/Anderson team holds a distant yet solid second place. Thanks to a great show in the last three holes, the team who traveled the furthest to get here, the Richardson/Baker team from Atlantic City, are in third place." Phil stopped himself, "Wait, Atlantic City? That's where Truman and the aliens met about the cardboard." Phil looked over at the Richardson/Baker twosome who, strangely, were carrying all their clubs in cardboard boxes. That was all Phil needed to see. He screamed, "Patrick turn the cameras off, they're aliens!" And with this comment, Phil and Patrick went running into the woods.

Eugene and I were standing by the clubhouse. A funny thing had happened ever since we'd teed off at hole one. People had started following us around. At first, there were just three or four people besides Eugene's and my parents, but by the time we got to hole four, at least half of the spectators in the crowd were watching us.

This was fine by me, because I was playing one of the best rounds of my life. After that first shot went awry, I quickly got back on track. Playing golf in front of all those people made my dreams come into focus. This was where I wanted to be—on the golf course. I knew being a professional golfer was a big dream, but I also knew that it was one that was worth chasing. My future started today. I was going to watch my diet again, head back to the weight room, be true to myself, and keep playing golf until I made it all the way.

And Eugene, well, he was playing in the youth tournament and everyone watching him couldn't stop talking about him. People said that he was probably one of the best junior golfers in the country! A huge smile had been plastered on his face ever since Mrs. Beltzendohoover let us enter the tournament. I felt like maybe, just maybe, with the way things were going today, Eugene would forgive me and we could be friends again.

"What do you think you're doing?" My happiness bubble suddenly popped as Calvin and Dave approached us.

"What do you mean?" I asked.

"This is supposed to be my tournament," said Calvin. "I'm supposed to be winning this thing. And I would be winning if it wasn't for you and Eugene entering at the last minute."

"It's no big deal," I said. "We're just having a good day. That's all, Calvin."

"Well, your good day is turning my good day into a bad day." Calvin was clearly upset.

I didn't know what to say. "C'mon Calvin, it's just a game."

"No it's not just a game. It's being a winner or being a loser. It's about having half of the people here follow you and Eugene around instead of watching me and Dave. It's about getting published in the sports section. It is not just a game," said Calvin. Man, this guy was such a jerk. How was I ever friends with him for so long?

"So what do you want me to do about it?" I asked.

"Start losing," said Calvin.

I let out a little laugh. "What?"

"You heard me. I want you guys to start losing. If Dave and I win every hole 'til the end, we'll tie for first. You guys wouldn't even have to lose. We'd all win."

Calvin's deal set something off inside of me. Who did Calvin think he was? Did he think he could just walk all over me and Eugene because he didn't like to lose? And because he's good at football and friends with the popular people I'm just supposed to let him do whatever he wants? And I was supposed to be his best friend? Wouldn't he want his best friend to win for a change? I looked over at Eugene. He was clearly uncomfortable. I looked back over to Calvin. This wasn't right.

"Get over yourself, Calvin. There's no chance we're gonna lose just because you want to win. We want to win too," I said.

Calvin stared hard into my face. For a minute there I thought he was going to punch me. But he didn't. "Fine, but our friendship's done, Jason. I hope you're happy with yourself now. C'mon Dave, let's get away from these nerds." Calvin and Dave walked away toward a group of cool people. I noticed Mark and Tommy in the group.

CHAPTER THIRTEEN

A BIZARRE FINISH

Things went fine for eight holes. Actually, they went better than fine. At first I thought that Eugene would be nervous after Calvin confronted us and that he would play poorly, but it was just the opposite. He was playing even better than before. I guess those goons weren't intimidating him anymore.

And I was playing great too. If Calvin's talk tried to make us nervous, it totally backfired. I was completely calm and even more determined not to let him win. My shots were going farther and I was concentrating like never before. I was in the zone. In fact, during the last eight holes or so, I think we had played more of my shots than Eugene's! I also sunk three or four pretty long putts.

Walking between holes, Eugene and I were talking the way we used to. Not just about the golf match, but also about regular stuff too. He updated me on the progress of his green lemon grass. "It's almost ready for the patent application process." We planned to get together on Sunday to continue our sock tournament where we left off three months ago. I even told Eugene about what it was like working in the deli and how I was approaching total mastery of slicing. It was almost like things were back to normal again. What was even better though, was that in about fifteen minutes, we were going to collect two big trophies and have our pictures taken for the newspaper.

By the time we got to hole eighteen, I had almost totally forgotten about what Calvin had said. We were three holes behind him and Dave, so they had already finished. We had a big group of people following us around, and it was easy to get caught up in the moment thinking that everything was fine. Things weren't fine, though.

Because we were winning by so many strokes coming up to hole eighteen, we basically just had to finish in order to win. There was no possibility that anyone could catch up with us. It was a done deal. I have never won anything in my life except for a video game, so I was pretty excited.

Since we were the last group to tee off in the beginning of the tournament, we were also the last group to finish. Ahead of us were the two "aliens" from Atlantic City. They were loading their clubs back into the cardboard boxes after finishing the last hole with a par. Phil was hiding in the woods behind them, taking photographs and trying to get hair samples. Everyone else had already finished, including Calvin and Dave. The crowd was bigger than ever as we came up for our final approach shot to the green. The fans applauded wildly for us as we walked up the fairway.

It was then, though, that it became clear just how desperate the cool kids had gotten. They couldn't handle losing to a fatso and a weirdo. Eugene was about to swing, when from out of nowhere, a golf cart came racing down the hill, heading right for him. Two people wearing those big socks you put over your clubs on their heads, were in the cart, speeding toward my partner. One guy was enormous and the other was tiny. *I wonder who it could be?*

Before Eugene swings he goes into this almost trance-like state of total concentration. He closes his eyes and takes a few deep breaths. He told me once he's able to actually see the path of the ball before he hits it. Being able to concentrate like that helps Eugene to be great at golf, but it doesn't help him at all when you're trying to get him to notice two people that are attacking him with a golf cart.

"Eugene!" I shouted. He didn't even look at me. He was concentrating too hard. He couldn't hear me. "Eugene!" I shouted again. "Eugene, look out!"

It was no use, Eugene was in another state. I ran over to try to push him out of the way, but I was all the way across the fairway and there was no way I was going to make it on time. Eugene was a sitting duck.

To the side of Eugene, the "aliens" from Atlantic City were eating a couple of hot dogs, completely unaware of the runaway golf cart. Phil, who was still spying on the supposed aliens from the woods, ran out onto the fairway while Patrick was still filming behind him. He wasn't going to reach Eugene in time either. So instead, he screamed at the aliens from Atlantic City. "Use your powers!" he shouted. Of course, they had no idea what he was talking about, but they were so scared by Phil running out of the woods straight at them that they started to run away from him. Instead, they banged right into Eugene and tumbled to the ground alongside him. A second later, the golf cart whizzed by the spot Eugene had been standing, missing all three of them by a hair.

With Eugene and the "aliens" from Atlantic City laying on the ground in the fairway, the golf cart veered sharply to the left, obviously caught off guard by missing Eugene. It ran out of control, ran straight through the crowd, and landed in the fountain. Harvey and Phil jumped into the water to catch the two masked riders. We all ran up to see what would happen next. Patrick was filming the whole thing.

Harvey and Phil easily handled the two villains. Harvey might be small, but he's strong. Phil was so much taller than anyone else that his arms were like vice grips. When they lifted the covers off their faces, Mark and Tommy were both crying. I knew that they were bad, but this was bad even for them. Tommy looked like a drowned weasel. Mark, for once in his life, looked scared. He was in big trouble now.

"I don't think you boys understand how much trouble you are both in," said Harvey. "What would cause you to do such a thing? Eugene never once wronged you. Do you know how badly you could have hurt him?" Harvey paused, looking around for someone to help him. "Dan?" he called out.

Dan, my boss at the sandwich shop and Harvey's good friend, stepped up from the crowd. "Yes?"

"Please go call the police."

"I'm on my way." Dan ran to the clubhouse, shedding

hair all over the eighteenth fairway on his way. Mark looked even more scared now. For once in his life, he wasn't going to be getting away with anything.

"Patrick, roll on me!" Phil shouted to Patrick. Patrick turned his camera on Phil, who looked even more ridiculous than before. His small suit was soaked and his hair was a stringy mess on his head, but he was taking his role as golf commentator as serious as ever. "Ladies and gentlemen, I'm coming to you live from a scandal that just rocked the golf world to its foundations. In this fountain behind me lie the remains of a golf cart and a failed effort to accost young golf star and local favorite Eugene Jewel. Luckily, two aliens from New Jersey knocked Eugene to the ground just before being crushed by a golf cart. What would cause two individuals to commit such a dastardly deed? Perhaps we will never know, but at the very least we can be thankful that no one was hurt." Phil looked over at Eugene, who was clutching his ankle. "Well, at least we can be thankful that no one was hurt *badly*."

In all the chaos, I'd forgotten about Eugene. He did fall to the ground pretty hard. I ran from the crowd over to him. He was wincing in pain and covered in ketchup and mustard from the two hot dogs that got loose in the collision.

"Are you okay?" I asked, a little out of breath from sprinting over to Eugene.

"I think so," said Eugene. "I landed on my ankle though."

"It looks like a mild sprain," said Dr. Jewel, Eugene's mother. "You'll be fine in a week or two, but you need to stay off that leg for a few days. Why would those boys do such a thing?" Dr. Jewel shook her head in disbelief. "Have they given you trouble before?"

Eugene's eyes started to well up with tears. I could tell it wasn't from the pain of his leg. He was doing his best to hold it in.

"Yes they have, Dr. Jewel," I said. "But I don't think they will ever again. At least not while I'm around."

Harvey had come over to see how Eugene was doing. "How are you, champ?"

"I'll be okay," said Eugene.

"It's just a sprain," Dr. Jewel spoke as she examined her son. "He should be back to his normal self in about two weeks."

"So he can't play?" I asked.

"It's okay, Jason. Why don't you finish it out for him?" Harvey spoke in a calming tone. He paused for a moment. "And while Eugene is healing, why don't you come back to work at the course? I'm sure that we can find a place for you when he gets better too."

I smiled. Everything was working out for me.

I helped Eugene up to his feet.

"Come on, partner, let's finish winning this thing," said Eugene.

"You got it, partner," I said, grabbing an eight iron and walking up to the ball.

Phil and Patrick rushed over behind me. "Well, folks, it's all come down to this. In an ending I'm sure no one ever imagined, Jason Green and Eugene Jewel are about to close out the youth tournament in probably the most bizarre finish in the history of the event.

"Jason Green has been playing a wonderful round. Right now he is one hundred and twenty-six yards away. He is in excellent position to get the ball on the green. We quiet as Jason prepares for his swing."

I looked down the fairway. Everything except the pin on the green faded away. The clouds parted and the sun shone brightly on a spot about two feet in front of the hole. That was my target.

I took my shot.

"And a beautiful shot from Jason Green. Perfect arc. Great distance. And what is this folks? The ball is heading straight for the green. Jason should be in excellent position for the birdie. But wait, the ball's still rolling…it's heading right for the hole! Oh my goodness folks, it went in! From one hundred and twenty-six yards out, the ball went in the hole!"

I pumped my fist high into the air and smiled. With a broken golf cart floating in the fountain over my left shoulder, a police car arriving on the scene in the parking lot behind me, and my partner hobbling next to me, I hit the greatest shot of my life. And that's how I came to win the Youth Pairs Tournament.

When the smoke cleared and I lifted my ball from the bottom of the cup and received my trophy, I was so excited that I even hugged Phil. (Although I think he was only hugging me to distract me, so Patrick could get a hair sample.) I may have won the tournament, but in Phil's eyes, there was still a good chance that I was an alien.

TEST YOURSELF...ARE YOU A PROFESSIONAL READER?

Chapter 1: Trouble on the Flight to Mars

Describe the Puyallup Fair. What is Jason's favorite thing about the fair?

What did Jason do to get kicked out of the Puyallup Fair?

According to Officer Armstrong, what did Jason do in addition to scaring a bunch of little girls?

ESSAY

In this chapter, Jason played a prank on two girls, which resulted in him getting ejected from the Puyallup Fair. Although it was an accident, he demolished much of the interior of the Flight to Mars as well. Why do you think Jason played this prank? Have you ever played a joke on someone that went too far or had a joke played on you? How does it feel to have someone play a prank on you?

Chapter 2: Green's on the Green

What was Jason's punishment for the prank he pulled on the Flight to Mars?

According to Jason, why is it a funny picture to see him and Calvin walking down the street together?

How does Jason get Mark Brotherton to stop yelling "Green's on the green?"

ESSAY

Jason says he has developed a strategy to divert attention away from his weight problem. What is this strategy? How does this strategy effect the way Jason feels about himself? What does the term self-confidence mean? Why is it important to be confident and believe in yourself?

Chapter 3: Whispering Canyon

Jason speaks to Eugene Jewel for the first time ever in this chapter. Describe Eugene.

According to Jason, what was the coolest thing about golf?

Why did Eugene remind Jason of his aunt's golden retriever, Buttons?

ESSAY

In this chapter, Jason tells us about the different types of kids that go to his middle school. Jason is being unfair when he categorizes his classmates as dorks, nerds, cool kids, jocks, jerks, band geeks, cheerleaders, brains, bullies, and brats. Why do you think categorizing your classmates is unfair? Do you think you fit into any of these categories? If so, which ones and why? If not, how would you describe yourself?

Chapter 4: The Answer's in the Bucket

What were the two things that Jason noticed about Harvey right away?

Harvey tells Jason that before he starts helping him out on the course, he has to answer a question. What is that question?

Describe the process by which Jason cleans golf balls with Phil.

ESSAY

Phil has some pretty strange theories about the world. He thinks that the government is run by a robotic president who is controlled secretly by aliens. Do you have any strange theories? Make up a theory using some of the following words: dogs, kindergarten, airplanes, shoelaces, genius, talking, helmets, asteroids, fireballs, crayons, and pencils. For example, "Some dogs are geniuses, they go to school at night when people are sleeping. They can talk to each other and fly airplanes too. Sometimes, they wear helmets."

Chapter 5: Glasses

Describe Mark Brotherton and Tommy Rigo.

What was in the plastic container that Eugene showed Jason?

After Phil tells Jason about his Harry Truman theory, he asks him to go on the back nine and look in the deep rough for lost balls. What does Phil say he will reward Jason with if he does a good job?

ESSAY

Jason just watched Eugene get harassed by Mark and Tommy and didn't do anything about it. Has there ever been a time in your life when you could have helped someone who was in trouble, but didn't? Explain what happened and why you didn't help. If you had to do it all over again, what would you do?

Chapter 6: Playing Golf

Describe the term "drive" as it relates to golf. What are the main goals when driving the ball?

Why does Jason like hole thirteen? What happens if you mess up on thirteen?

Jason finds a golf club in the pond and holds it in his hands. Has he ever held a golf club before? When?

ESSAY

After Jason hits a few of Phil's golf balls into the pond, Harvey catches him. Instead of being angry with him, he offers to teach him how to play golf. Jason gets excited about this and agrees to stay two hours after work to watch people tee off on the first hole. How do you think this will help Jason's golf game? Have you ever learned something from watching someone? Explain.

Chapter 7: My First Lesson

Phil tells Jason that a platypus is not an animal. According to Phil, what is a platypus and how did they end up on earth?

Describe the first foursome that tees off when Jason is watching. What were the nicknames Jason gave each twosome?

What were the conclusions Jason made about golf after watching people tee off for a few hours?

ESSAY

Jason learns a great deal about the game of golf in this chapter. He discovers that he really likes golf. Do you have a favorite sport? What is it? What do you like about it? Describe your favorite moment playing or watching this sport.

Chapter 8: The Real Jason Green

What does Jason see in front of him when he finally responds correctly to Harvey's question?

According to the author of a golf book Jason read, why does a golfer need to lift weights?

Name a few things that Jason and Eugene would do when they hung out together.

ESSAY

Through his friendship with Eugene, Jason discovers that the cool crowd isn't always that cool. More importantly he learns a lot about himself and what he really thinks is cool. What is the meaning of the title of the chapter "The Real Jason Green?" Do you ever act differently to try to fit into the cool crowd? If not, why not? If so, what are you really like?

Chapter 9: A Dream is Born

According to Harvey, why is golf the hardest game in the world?

What is the Invitational Classic? What is the Youth Pairs Tournament?

Why doesn't Eugene like to play golf in front of people? What happened when Harvey entered him in a tournament in Tacoma?

ESSAY

Although Eugene doesn't initially want to play in the Youth Pairs Tournament, Jason eventually convinces him to. What do you think inspired Eugene to want to play? Has there ever been a time in your life when you didn't want to do something and somebody convinced you to do it? What happened?

Chapter 10: The Mini-Golf Disaster

What disturbing sight did Jason see when he rounded the corner on hole seven when he was playing mini-golf with Eugene?

According to Jason, why had this been the happiest six months of his life?

What does Harvey say to Jason when he shows up to work after the mini-golf disaster?

ESSAY

Jason asks himself a number of tough questions after he humiliates Eugene in favor of the cool crowd, such as, "Was fitting in that important to me? Important enough to hurt a friend?" These are interesting questions. As a young person, why do you think there is so much pressure to fit in? What does fitting in mean to you? Why is not fitting in brave sometimes? Can it be cool to not fit in?

Chapter 11: Let's Do It

What were Jason's responsibilities at Dan's Sandwiches?

What is Eugene referring to when he tells Jason, "I saw you?"

How does Jason stand up for Eugene and make things right between them?

ESSAY

Although Jason did some bad things to Eugene earlier in this story, he redeems himself by standing up for Eugene, who decides to give Jason a second chance. Why is it important to give people second chances? Have you ever been given a second chance? Have you ever given someone else a second chance?

Chapter 12: Kicking Butt

What happened on Jason's first shot of the tournament?

What was Mark Brotherton doing when Jason stared over at him after Eugene nailed a twenty-foot putt for birdie on the first hole?

Why does Phil think that two of the young golfers are aliens?

ESSAY

Playing, and winning, in a golf tournament with Eugene as his partner instead of Calvin, is a sign of how much Jason has changed since the beginning of this book. Jason's reaction to Calvin asking him to purposely lose the tournament is another sign of this change. Describe some of the differences between Jason at the beginning of the book and Jason at this point in the book. What is the biggest change you have ever gone through? Explain.

Chapter 13: A Bizarre Finish

While walking between holes at the Youth Pairs Tournament, Jason and Eugene began to talk the way they used to. What did they talk about?

What injury did Eugene sustain when he barely averted the golf cart that was headed right for him?

Why does Jason say that Phil hugged him when his final shot landed in the cup?

ESSAY

Congratulations! You have completed another Scobre book in the Dream Series. What did you learn from Jason's life? Are you like Jason in any way? What would you have done differently than Jason did in this book? How are you going to use this story to help you achieve your dreams?